THE DOLL

ALSO BY ISMAIL KADARE

The General of the Dead Army
The Siege
Chronicle in Stone
Twilight of the Eastern Gods
The File on H
The Three-Arched Bridge
Broken April
The Ghost Rider
The Concert
The Palace of Dreams
The Pyramid
Three Elegies for Kosovo
Spring Flowers, Spring Frost
Agamemnon's Daughter
The Successor
The Fall of the Stone City
The Accident
A Girl in Exile
The Traitor's Niche

Ismail Kadare

THE DOLL

A Portrait of My Mother

Translated from the Albanian
by John Hodgson

Harvill *Secker*
LONDON

1 3 5 7 9 10 8 6 4 2

Harvill Secker, an imprint of Vintage,
20 Vauxhall Bridge Road,
London SW1V 2SA

Harvill Secker is part of the Penguin Random House group of companies
whose addresses can be found at global.penguinrandomhouse.com

Penguin
Random House
UK

First published by Harvill Secker in 2020
First published by Onufri in Albania in 2015 with the title *Kukulla*

A CIP catalogue record for this book is
available from the British Library

penguin.co.uk/vintage

ISBN 9781787300934

Co-funded by the
Creative Europe Programme
of the European Union

The European Commission support for the production of this
publication does not constitute an endorsement of the contents
which reflects the views only of the authors, and the Commission
cannot be held responsible for any use which may be made
of the information contained therein.

Typeset in 12.5/18pt Adobe Garamond Pro Jouve (UK), Milton Keynes
Printed and bound in Great Britain by Clays Ltd, Elcograf S.p.A.

Penguin Random House is committed to a sustainable future for
our business, our readers and our planet. This book is made
from Forest Stewardship Council® certified paper.

MIX
Paper from
responsible sources
FSC® C018179

THE DOLL

IN APRIL 1994, my brother called from Tirana to tell me my mother was not expected to last.

Helena and I left on the first plane from Paris, hoping to arrive before it was too late. We found her still alive, but unable to understand anything. She lay in a coma in my aunt's apartment on Qemal Stafa Street, where she had been brought a few weeks before.

My cousin Besnik Dobi had carried her to her sister's in his own arms. He told us why he'd chosen to move her in this way, over the short distance from Dibra Street to the foot of Qemal Stafa, adding, 'Besides, she was very light.'

He tried to explain in more detail, repeating more or less the same thing. 'Incredible, how light she was! As if made of paper.'

Like a paper doll.

I wasn't sure if he had uttered these words or I had thought them myself, but they came as no surprise, as if I were hearing something I already knew.

A familiar scene passed through my mind: our daughters playing Doll with my mother. She would sit patiently between them while they fixed all kinds of ribbons and pins to her hair, saying the whole time, 'Granny, don't move.'

These scenes distressed Helena, but our daughters wouldn't listen. 'Granny doesn't complain,' they kept saying. 'Why should you?'

Lightness. The wooden stairs of the house, usually so sensitive, never creaked under her feet. Like her steps, everything about her was light – her clothes, her speech, her sighs.

Around the neighbourhood and later at school, we learned all those poems about mothers. There were also poems, and even a song, about children who didn't have mothers, with heart-rending repetitions of the phrase 'without a mother'. I didn't know of any classmates who didn't have a mother. Perhaps there were some, but they didn't mention it. According to one school friend, not having a mother was shameful, but a friend from Form B said that not having a father was shameful. Two of our girl friends, Ylberja and Ela Laboviti, laughed at both of them, and said they were mixing up the words 'shame' and 'pity' and didn't know what they were talking about.

This question of a mother involved more than just whether you had one. You might sing all day about your beloved mother, 'the finest in the world, how sweet her fragrance, tra la la', but still this wasn't enough. Some children worried, although they wouldn't admit it, that their mothers didn't look as young as others, or were even old.

But this was no great disaster compared to the case of the school in the next neighbourhood, where no fewer than two mothers were separated from their husbands, or the case of Pani X., who arrived in tears because someone had called him a 'son of a whore' on the way to school; he could only be consoled when Ylberja and Ela Laboviti explained that this meant nothing, because people who used these words about anyone's mother were themselves possibly no better than they should be.

I realised very quickly that I too had a problem with my mother, but of a very different kind. It had to do mainly with her fragility, with what would later strike me as her resemblance to paper or plaster of Paris. At first dimly, but with increasing clarity, I understood that the maternal things mentioned in the poems and songs – milk, breasts, fragrance and the warmth – were hard to relate to my own mother.

It was not a matter of coldness. Her sensitivity was evident, and her caring nature too. Something else was missing, and I came to realise that it had to do with her self-restraint, her inability to cross a certain barrier.

In short, from an early age I felt that my mother was less like the mothers in the poems and more a kind of draft mother or an outline sketch which she could not step beyond. Even her white face had the frozen and inscrutable quality of a mask, especially when glazed with panstick as she had learned from Kiko Pinoja, the famous make-up artist of the brides of Gjirokastra, whose house was almost adjacent to our own. Later, when on a trip to Japan I saw a performance of kabuki for the first time, the whiteness of the actors' faces seemed familiar to me. They contained the same secret as my mother's, a doll-like mystery, but without terror.

Similarly, her tears flowed like those in cartoon films. I rarely knew what lay behind them, just as I couldn't understand how for years I never once saw her entering or leaving the toilet, as if she never went there.

Mothers are the hardest creatures to understand, Andrei Voznesensky said to me at Alain Bosquet's in Paris, during a dinner which Helena and I had been invited to. I had asked the Russian poet, among other things, about a famous poem of his, written partly as an anagram. It included a line in which the Russian for 'mother' – *mat* – was repeated three times, *matmatmat*, but left unfinished on the fourth repetition – *ma* – which at the end, associated with the *t* of the third *mat* ('mother'), made the word *tma*, meaning 'darkness'.

Voznesensky was in very low spirits at that dinner, and to me this seemed to influence his interpretation of these lines. It was my first and last meeting with him, so I had no chance to further explore what he meant. But his explanation, more or less, involved a connection between the words 'mother' and 'darkness', because a child emerges from its mother's womb as if out of darkness: an endless cycle of *matma*, 'motherdarkness', in which both the mother and the darkness remain beyond understanding.

If I found it difficult to understand the cause of my mother's tears, this was not the case with her boredom. She told me the reason herself in a phrase that terrified me the first time I heard it, and it still makes my skin creep to recall it: 'The house is eating me up!'

I soon realised that this was quite an ordinary way of saying that you're bored at home. But I had long been obsessed with working out the meaning of words, and I tormented myself with the most horrible visions. How dreadful it would be if the house you lived in ate you up.

2

MY MOTHER, otherwise so hard to fathom, made no secret of her absolute dislike for our house.

This was perhaps an understandable reaction for a seventeen-year-old bride entering this vast building. Her first thought, if only in passing, would have been that a house like ours would take such a lot of work – especially for a girl who, as I later learned from her sisters' stories, had often been scolded for a lack of housewifely zeal. Besides, she was the sole young wife, with no prospects of a second bride in the household, because my father was an only son, and fatherless.

The house was not merely huge, but ancient and oppressive. Moreover, her mother-in-law, my future grandmother, had a reputation both for tight-lipped severity and for wisdom. It would be a long time before I understood the profound reasons why reputations for great wisdom so irritated my mother.

The first chilliness between the young bride and her mother-in-law was probably caused by the bride's lack of interest in the house, or rather her failure to be awed by it. But the true cause lay deeper, making their coldness unavoidable.

It was well known that when the families of Gjirokastra formed marriage alliances, they immediately redefined their relationships to each other. Besides the usual forging of a bond between two clans, there was an extraordinary kind of deafening din in the period before the wedding. This was an opportunity for the old houses to behave with their well-known swank, pride, swagger and vanity, so that the two families being joined in marriage could be set on the scales and compared. During the long winter nights, the future brides, and indeed the grooms, would hear all kinds of insinuations about the other party: 'They think they're a cut above us,' and the like. It was a kind of cold war that burdened both sides, especially the young brides and their mothers-in-law, with feelings of contempt for one another.

So, whether or not my future mother expressed her disdain for the Kadare house, or my grandmother pursed her lips at her, an inescapable frostiness set in between the two.

As the years passed, and with great difficulty, I would come to understand – or more accurately, think I understood – the senseless history of the supposed animosity between the Kadares and the Dobis.

This ill will that initially seemed quite inevitable became complicated and later beyond comprehension. Then the opposite happened: the fog lifted of a sudden, and everyone said, 'So that's what this business was all about! We were too blind to see it.'

The hostility arose from the impossibility of comparing the two families, starting with their houses, which were so different that it was hard to believe they belonged to the same city.

Our house was old and grim, but that of my grandfather on my mother's side was the opposite. It was large, but it had neither deep cellars nor a cistern, nor fancy wooden stairs, not to mention uninhabited rooms, a prison, secret subterranean passages and useless corridors and vestibules. The Dobi house had its particular character because it stood on its own, not on a street or in a neighbourhood that would require it to fit in with other houses. It occupied an empty space beside the castle and a swift-flowing stream. In the absence of secrets, it possessed a patch of land that might be considered a garden, which also contained a small house known as the outbuilding, in which there lived a Roma family, former servants of the Dobis.

But instead of restoring the equilibrium between the houses, everybody made matters worse. The Kadares and the Dobis, as I learned later, differed from one another even more than their houses did. The most striking contrast was that most of the Dobi family were alive, while most Kadares were dead. Now and then I would find an old photograph tucked away in the house and run to my grandmother to ask who this person was and where I could find them. Her answer always saddened me. 'What about this one?' I would ask a few days later when I found another photograph. But the answer was the same: they were no longer of this world.

There were plenty of other differences. The Dobi house had trees and birds, violins and Roma. There were the Greek peasants on my grandfather's former properties, and my maternal aunts and uncles – *tezet* and *ungjët* – but the problem was that these things were not in any way comparable to what we Kadares had. Could you compare, for instance, skill with the violin to the two rooms that we were not allowed to enter – or the dungeon, as the prison was called? And I knew that we couldn't have *tezet* and *ungjët*, because, according to my grandmother, in our house they wouldn't be sisters and brothers of our mother, but of our father, and the offspring of our grandmother herself, and we would use different words for them.

Later, when both Dobi uncles went abroad to study, one to Budapest and the other to Moscow, the difference between them and us was more evident in the letters that they sent from far away than in their actual absence. In our house, letters never arrived from anybody, and to me this seemed normal, because everybody knew that the dead didn't send them.

The Doll (for this sobriquet was now, if not replacing the word 'mother', at least relegating it to second place) would have found it hard to put into words, but she had known that she would have to face up to the Kadare house, with its high windows, cupboards, porches, secret chambers, carved wooden ceilings and famous dungeon, and all those forebears with sonorous names, Seit Kadare, Avdo Kadare, Shahin Kadare, and the most renowned among them, Ismail Kadare, my great-great-grandfather, who, as I liked to recall, had become famous in a song, not for killing Turks, as one would expect, but because of his clothes, or rather his pursuit of fashion.

Against this menacing pile of stone, the Doll had her own army of trees, birds, violins, sisters and former servants. At first sight she appeared fragile and naive, but she too had her secrets. The Doll did not know many things, but she was clearly aware of the truth behind the mundane but slippery phrase 'financial situation'. The Dobis were well-to-do – that is, rich – and the Kadares were not.

This fact was never mentioned in either of the

two houses, as if it were agreed upon that each side should wear a mask. Under their mask of modest tastes in everything, the Dobis concealed their wealth. And in turn the Kadares wore a mask of grandeur to cover their poverty.

The alliance between the two was a mistake from the start, and nobody ever understood the reason for the marriage.

3

HOWEVER HARD I tried, I could not picture the Doll entering her husband's house as a bride in 1933. Something always got in the way, a fog that fell across either her description or my imagination. What route did she follow? It was easy to think of the party of wedding guests setting off on the main road from the bride's father's house at the foot of the castle, and later, in the centre of the city, descending the steep hill of Varosh from the 'Crest of the Market'. The scene became surreal on the street that led to our own house, by Dr Vasil Laboviti's, where in 1943 he was to inexplicably host a dinner for the Germans. First was the house of the doctor, whose daughter was in the same class as myself, and further down the road was the house of Pavli Ura, another class-mate, whose surname derived from a bridge, an *urë*, whether real or bogus nobody knew. There was a great torrent of water that gushed out, but there was no bridge anywhere, and Pavli Ura himself was unable to explain his own surname. Meanwhile, a few paces further on, in front of the Fico house, nobody referred any more to the bridge but to 'Fico's stream'.

The Fico house was not only large but perhaps the most beautiful in the city, and some said that this was why it had produced the most famous foreign minister in Albanian history. How easy it was to imagine a building with this reputation giving its name to a stream. A stretch of the road ran alongside this stream as far as Kako Pino's house, the dream home of all the city's future brides – small, romantic and full of vases of flowers, and almost attached to ours. In front of the gates to the two houses rose the crooked, wayward Lunatics' Lane, a street unlike any other.

All these things must have made an impression on the Doll, who was not without curiosity. However, they paled in comparison with other riddles. Of the three great unknowns that awaited her – husband, house and mother-in-law – it was probably the last that inspired the greatest fear. She had only seen her future husband once, from the window of her house shortly before the wedding. Before that, a distant cousin had brought a photograph of her future home, along with the rumours that circulated about it. Of these, the most mysterious was the matter of the prison. As far as was known, the Kadare house was one of the four or five houses in the city that had a prison. For some this fact was plain madness, but for others it evoked certain long-obsolete conceptions of the law. In other words, the state had laws, and so did the house. In short, each took care of its own.

For the Doll, her mother-in-law was the real enigma. Besides the qualities summed up in the pitiless description 'tight-lipped and wise', there was also the question of whether she left the house or not, to which the answer was not altogether clear. The belief had arisen that if the lady of the Kadare household had not yet declared that she would never again leave her gates, then she was preparing to do so.

The custom of elderly women not leaving the house was one of the city's most puzzling traditions. Nobody knew the reason for it, or even its origin or the event that had prompted it. A certain lady would announce one day that she would leave the house no more, and nobody would ask why or wherefore.

But it was certain that not going out was a matter of status, a sort of promotion, and rather chic.

I don't think the Doll would have thought much

about the deep meaning or otherwise of her mother-in-law not leaving the house. If anything, she may have thought it would be better for her mother-in-law to go out instead of shutting herself up at home. But there is no doubt that the Doll, as she was getting ready to climb the stairs to the big drawing room in her new home on the first morning after the wedding, would have felt that her hardest trial was not the clamour of the celebrations, nor her first night with her husband, but rather her presentation before the pitiless jury of the women of the house.

Cold, sitting in a row, dressed in black, with their coffee cups resting on the window ledges, and with eyes that forgave nothing, they followed her every movement.

The Doll had no doubt been taught how to behave, but it is probable that at that moment she was too flustered to remember the advice. The lorgnettes in the ladies' hands were a real surprise to her. As if their ice-cold eyes were not enough, they extended to one another those treacherous lorgnettes, through which first one and then another stared into the distance.

A moment would have come when the Doll thought they might turn their lorgnettes on her, with the words, 'Ah, so this is the bride, let's look at her more closely . . .'

It is likely that the curiosity shown by this inspection through the lorgnettes was one of the first things the Doll related on her first visit home to her parents.

This visit usually took place one week after the wedding and was for some reason called 'the maiden's dinner', and it was certainly more important than any dinner or festival that followed.

On such an occasion, an experienced eye could gather many things from the face of a girl who had just been transformed into a bride: pleasure, disappointment, perplexity . . . rarely happiness. It was a unique infiltration into the opposite camp, a parley of both intelligence and counter-intelligence.

Even if it did not take a dramatic turn, when for instance the bride claimed refuge in her father's home, this first communication from 'the other side' played an important role. The later attitude to the rival household, the strategy in matters purposely left unfinished – files on property or inheritance, for example – might depend on this visit home so fallaciously entitled 'the maiden's dinner'. This visit might set in motion the kind of covert diplomacy for which the old Gjirokastra houses were famous. Go-betweens who were used to these delicate matters, and let their remarks fall here and there as if by chance, might comment favourably or not on promises made earlier, such as the possibility of a long-term loan for repairs to the Kadare house.

It is hard to discern if this phase of the Doll's life, which might be called her Mata Hari period, introduced any complication into relations between the two families.

According to what little she told me, she had

no rapport of any kind with the other people of the household, apart from her little sister. Her two brothers always had their minds elsewhere, because they were both preparing to enter the *lycée*. Later they read the city newspaper *Demokratia* and talked about totally incomprehensible things such as the theories of Freud or Branko Merxhani, and prisoners of a new kind who had recently become fashionable, whom they called 'political prisoners'.

Her brothers' opinions increasingly diverged from everyone else's. When the Doll told them of the ladies' lorgnettes, they laughed impatiently. According to them, the Kadare ladies used them to show off, because all the old families of Gjirokastra suffered from delusions of grandeur.

Later, they ascribed the old mother-in-law's decision not to leave the house to the same reason. According to them, all these crazy customs were a way of increasing authority. My elder uncle, who was in a higher class, added something that he had apparently read, and which I did not understand, about 'exteriorising death', or distancing it from you, as one might say.

I have tried to imagine the Doll's maiden's dinner: in her father's house, they did not hide the fact that they had been anxious, so their first questions were whether her husband had behaved properly, or blundered in some way. Her sisters asked other questions, of the most naive sort, such as whether she had tried to look through a lorgnette, and whether 'she' – her mother-in-law – was really as wise as they said. Other questions would be uttered in a whisper and not in front of her parents.

The two days of her visit passed quickly, and the Doll set off just as she had arrived, escorted by Vito, a neighbourhood gypsy.

It was natural that the Kadare house, no longer seen through a bridal veil, would look different, bigger and more mysterious.

Whatever her mother-in-law's expression may

have been, frowning or smiling, it will have looked questioning, as she imagined what the young bride had been doing back home with her own family, what questions they had asked, what they had wanted to find out.

Throughout that week, so different to the previous one, the Doll must have felt homesick, and perhaps less secure.

Once, taking advantage of my grandmother's absence from the room, she had taken up a lorgnette left by the window and put it to her eyes. As she said later, she thought that she would see Greece . . . And at the same time perhaps she would understand those faraway things that her mother-in-law and her mother-in-law's friends talked about: the English, the war, Hitler . . .

4

HOUSES LIKE ours seemed constructed with the specific purpose of preserving coldness and misunderstanding for as long as possible. When I first dimly felt this, I must have been five or six years old. As so often with things I didn't like or which frightened me, I at once started imagining ways to get round these feelings; I almost persuaded myself that everything would be different if our house were smaller, with only one storey, or without secret recesses I was forbidden to enter, not to mention the cellars, the cistern and the dungeon.

For years on end I witnessed the frostiness between my grandmother and the Doll, so it wasn't hard for me to imagine what had happened in the early period of her marriage.

For a time the irritation between them did not show, but this delay did not offer any kind of hope. It was like the familiar expression just before the onset of winter, 'how nice that the weather is holding', which people say while also not expecting that winter will not come.

The frigidity and hostility gradually increased. After the first defeats of the Doll's army, as I liked to think of her resources in this battle – flowers, music, gypsies and all the rest – she called upon her secret weapon, her last hope: the superiority that came from her wealth. But this too was defeated.

It was in this state of panic that, instead of the Doll surrendering, something happened which was truly unforeseen.

It was at once a source of amazement, terror, delight and scandal.

It was a trial.

A trial within the Kadare household.

A trial of an insoluble case.

The whole thing took place in secret. Some relatives knew about it, but nobody could believe what was happening. They thought of the trial as the sort of mischief that sometimes took place in Gjirokastra. Perhaps the Kadares thought up this escapade because they already had a dungeon inside their house. Our prison is ready, why shouldn't we hold a trial?

Other people viewed it from a kind of psychophilosophical angle, as something influenced by the legal environment in which my father had spent his entire life, as the fulfilment of the dream of an ordinary civil servant who, although coming from an old legal family, had remained a simple court summoner.

Time would show that what happened was neither a jolly prank nor a symptom of schizophrenia. Gradually, as I grew up, it became clear to me that a legal process was taking place in our house, and that it had started before I was born. The astonishing thing was that as time passed, this 'process', instead of appearing grotesque, acquired a deeper meaning in my eyes.

The questions of what this trial was, why it was being held, who was the judge and who was being convicted, troubled me for a long time.

Finally I grasped that trials of this kind recurred time after time. The judge was my father and the defendants were two women: my formidable grandmother faced by the Doll, her antithesis. The trials were always over the same issue: the coldness and misunderstanding in the Kadare house. In other words, the acrimony between a mother and her daughter-in-law.

At first, like many others, I could easily have said that my father had lost his wits. Later I became curious less about my father's madness than something else: his hesitation. This involved the initial question of what sort of trial this was. If a trial was taking place over something, the judge was trying to identify a culprit. My father was undecided; he was in two minds.

The case was not at all as simple as it first appeared. My father was hesitating about something that many people would be totally sure of. In other words, when he came back from work and saw the enraged faces of his mother and his bride, the natural thing to do would be to immediately blame the young wife – especially as his mother was a grand old lady of the Kadares who for years had not deigned to step foot outside her house, a house dating back to 1700, if not 1600, and who, since her husband, Shahin Kadare the judge, departed this world, had nobody but her only son, and had been famed for her wisdom ever since the time when her father-in-law Ismail Kadare had been mentioned in a famous song . . .

Now, regardless of all this, her only son was doing something unprecedented, setting her on the scales against her daughter-in-law, to judge which of the two was in the right.

'My son has gone mad.' If she didn't utter these words out loud, she no doubt whispered them to her sister, Nesibe Karagjozi, who came to visit twice a week, and after her to Auntie Xhemo, and then to other women friends, including the shades of the dead, to whom she perhaps told everything in even greater detail.

As I grew up, I came to understand her anxiety better. An earthquake would have shaken us less than this shock delivered by my father. In the *lycée*, I racked my brains over this, while life went on as before. Under the influence of my reading, I understood that some surprising event, a turning point, was in the offing.

However, while I could imagine my grand-mother's fear, I could not at all understand what the Doll might be feeling. Later, when I thought back to this long story, especially when both were dead, I was sure that the Doll's idiosyncratic character must have helped her through this muddle. It even occurred to me that from that time I began to discern that the Doll had her own way of inspiring dread: a mixture of coldness and plaster-whiteness, a riddle like the masks of Japanese theatre or Voznesensky's *matmatma*, in which a mother and darkness become one.

This did not prevent me from looking for the cause of what had happened in a more tangible and less metaphysical form. Sooner or later, my mind hit upon that which, as they say, explains the inexplicable: love.

I would have been astonished if someone had told me this at the time. I knew nothing about my mother's private life, and would scarcely have imagined even the slightest kind of love affair before her engagement, until one day she herself told me something. It was the first time that the Doll confided in me.

Izmini Kokobobo, a cousin of ours who followed fashion and liked to tease the Doll, would have burst out laughing to hear this event described as 'a crush'. It was nothing of the sort.

A short time before the Doll's engagement, the three Dobi sisters were at a wedding where my mother's future fiancé was expected to appear among the guests. The sisters were looking out for him from a window of the house, until one of them said, 'Look, there he is, with the black Borsalino.' The Doll's heart dropped into the pit of her stomach. They had told her that her fiancé was handsome and tall, but the man in the Borsalino was stout, rotund. The Doll wanted to weep, but her little sister called out, 'Wait, you fool, that's not him. It's the other one, on the right.'

The Doll described how her heart returned to its proper place. She didn't sleep that night from joy.

I was at high school when she told me this story. During dinner, I said to her, 'Mama, tell me how you fell in love with Father when you saw him from the window.'

The Doll was embarrassed. 'Why, was that love?' she muttered.

'Real love,' my sister and I said, almost in the same voice. 'Love at first sight,' I went on. 'That's what it's called. We've had it in class. Dante and Beatrice.'

My father listened with complete indifference, as if we were talking about someone else.

It was the first and last time that such a thing was mentioned. I knew nothing about, nor could I imagine, their intimacy together.

A short time before the Doll passed away, she told me that she had something to ask of me. As she spoke, her voice faltered. She wanted to be buried in the same grave as 'him', meaning her husband.

'Smajl, don't laugh,' she said. And she explained that she was frightened of being alone under the earth.

I gave my word that I would do as she said.

Later, when I dealt with this matter, which was

not easy, because the laws and regulations changed every year, I could not help wondering whether this could really be called a love story, even a simple one: seeing a man from a window and then, three-quarters of a century later, wanting to be with him in the same grave.

I became certain that this was indeed a love story, with a beginning and an end, like the Russian poet's *matma*, or rather like those two *ma*s with the letter *t* in between, belonging to both mother and darkness.

Or so I told myself. Nevertheless, when I thought of the well-known house trials, I thought that even if the story involving a window and a death were true, it might explain many things but never the mystery of my father's behaviour. ('These brides nowadays, they know a few wiles that drive poor men out of their minds . . .' After these words, my grandmother's friends fixed their eyes on the old lady, but she, cold and disdainful, pretended not to understand. This business of 'wiles' not only failed to make me curious, but frightened me, because it seemed to belong to that secret aspect of the Doll.)

In short, neither romantic love nor feminine wiles explained my father's surprising behaviour, because such things were extremely ephemeral. Whereas the never-ending chronicle of the trials in our house was the very opposite of ephemeral.

The ritual had continued unchanged for years. Sometimes one side won the case, and sometimes the other. The traces of tears on the Doll's cheeks showed when she lost, and a spring in her step indicated the opposite. In the latter case, my grandmother withdrew spitefully to the second floor and did not come down for days on end.

One day, quite by chance, it seemed the mystery that had tortured me for years had suddenly become clear.

I do not remember why I'd been angry with the Doll, probably over my books, because I always became irritated when they were moved. I spoke harsh words, while she listened to me with a guilty look. I asked how she could possibly have failed to learn that my books must not be moved, and still she watched me with her bewildered gaze, as she always did when books were the subject. I must have repeated two or three times the words 'how . . . possibly' when she replied, 'That's what I'm like.'

I don't know what was special in her voice that made such an impression on me, but I felt my anger subside as I went on about the books without looking at her, and asked, 'What do you mean?'

There was no answer. Then, when I repeated the question, in a faint voice she said, 'Well, sort of . . . you know yourself, I'm not very clever.'

'Really,' I said. 'Who told you that? Izmini Kokobobo?'

I uttered these words without lifting my head, as if I were frightened of seeing the tears in her eyes.

She did not reply, perhaps emotion prevented her, and I did not provoke her further.

Suddenly I felt a pang of tenderness as never

before. I was fifteen years old and had never thought that a twinge of this kind could be so impossible to withstand. And with it, other things that I'd had occasion to feel, but had refused to make conscious, rushed into my mind and appeared with lightning clarity. These things had to do with the Doll's unfounded naivety, with her extended adolescence, which made her unaware of many things, or mistaken in her interpretation of them. Perhaps this was why so much emphasis was placed on my grandmother's wisdom, which caused the Doll so much suffering. And perhaps . . . and this was the main thing . . . here lay the answer to the riddle of my father's behaviour. Since the first days of their marriage, he had probably felt that same tenderness I had. And it had been neither advice from his teachers nor his reading of the newspaper *Demokratia* which he carried in his jacket pocket every day, like the judges and lawyers he worshipped, but a corrosive feeling, unlike anything else in the world, that would drive him to overturn the habits of the three-hundred-year-old house of the Kadares and resort to . . . a trial.

The trial was in fact between his mother and his wife, and would determine who was right: his mother, his wife, both, or neither!

Defend the Doll, if necessary! From him, her husband, in all circumstances! Whenever and wherever. To the grave . . .

5

I HAD NOTICED that each member of our family
had a unique relationship to the house. My grandmother's was the most natural and obvious. One
had the impression that long ago she had established
a rapport with its archways, rafters and buttresses.
The decision not to leave the house was evidently
part of a process of becoming absorbed into it.

My father's own alliance with the house was
strong but entirely different, founded on what had
become the sole passion of his life: repairing it.
For him everything else took second place. This

was so generally known that when in our history class the teacher spoke to us about the great rebuilding undertaken by Marcus Aurelius, Ela Laboviti whispered to me from the next bench, 'Just like your father!'

I became increasingly sure that all this was more than a matter of repairs. It was probably connected to his authority, and, looking at it this way, one might say that my father, in attempting to fix the house, was merely trying to restore his own dominance.

As one can imagine, the Doll's connection to the house could only be superficial. She continued to be distressed by the size of the rooms, and indifferent if not hostile to repairs. Her expression 'the house eats you up' had earlier made me curious, because I could not tell which torture would be worse, being gnawed at slowly day by day, or gobbled up all at once. Now the phrase had acquired a third meaning, the truest and most dramatic of them all: poverty.

My father's weakness for repairs was also the main reason for our financial straits. My uncles openly teased him and would ask me, 'What's the Great Repairer up to? Planning an interior triumphal arch?'

I didn't know how to reply. My grandmother had explained to me that my father worried about repairs more than he should, but there was no getting away from them.

If each person had their own special bond with the house, my relationship was the least clear of all. It was hard to explain because there were no words for it. Either I didn't know them, or they weren't yet invented.

It was easy for instance to talk about the house of the big doctor Laboviti, where our entire class had gone to wish Ela a happy birthday. Everyone said how beautiful it was inside. Or how warm. And if some thoughts were left unspoken, we all knew that they had to do with the notorious dinner for the Germans. Whereas it was hard to say things like this about our house, where the class also came to congratulate me on my birthday. It was even hard to guess what my schoolmates' private thoughts were. I remember that when Kiço Rexha begged me in a whisper to tell him the whereabouts of the dungeon, as he called the prison, I nodded in its direction, but when he asked if my father had ever put me into it, I answered no, and at the same time felt insulted.

If anyone had asked me what my house looked like, I wouldn't have known how to reply. This stemmed from a feeling that I dared not confess to anyone. A part of the house appeared to me . . . unreal. This was not a matter of imagination and fantasy, but of totally tangible spaces. On the second floor for instance, behind the room with the fireplace, or the winter room, as we called it, there were two unfinished partitions left after the most recent repair of 1936. I had long understood that every repair project spawned one or two more rooms – or the reverse, swallowed a couple. Shut up with temporary doors, nailed with two crossed planks, these chambers always attracted me. Beyond the planks, you could see rafters and half-finished windows in a beautiful, soft, falling light, especially in the afternoon.

These were not yet rooms but 'sort of' and 'not yet' spaces, and nameless embryos of this kind filled our house. The summer room. The winter corner. The balcony room. The big gallery, or the little gallery.

I was impatient for these rooms to be born, after such a long gestation, even as I realised that my father's sole desire in life, the next repair, would never be totally fulfilled.

My grandmother was to die in 1953, my father in 1975, and the Doll in 1994. The house itself would unexpectedly cease to exist in 1999. During the war, when German-occupied Gjirokastra was bombed by the English, I heard a lot about its possible destruction from the air. People said that two bombs from a heavy English bomber could raze to the ground this three-hundred-year-old house, which seemed so indestructible.

Ever since then, I seem always to glimpse in the sky an English aircraft, blindly but insistently looking for . . .

To get back to the story of the Doll, I remember a phrase written on the wall by the not-yet-annexes, a favourite place of mine to leave notes, in the shape of half a line of verse, or rather the name of a girl from Form B, whom I was sure I would never forget.

The phrase 'If Izmini Kokobobo did not exist . . .' was incomplete, but I knew what was missing. If Izmini Kokobobo did not exist, the Doll would feel better.

This seemed cynical. Perhaps this was why the phrase was left unfinished. But its meaning was less cynical than it was grotesque.

Izmini Kokobobo was a cousin of ours who had returned from Italy. She was one of the girls of the city who had interrupted her studies in 1939 in protest against the Italian invasion. Later, for the same reason, she had joined the partisans, ending up with an official position under the new regime. She was the only person who, when she came on business to Gjirokastra, stayed with us instead of in chilly hotels. She brought news from the capital city, and also her roaring laughter, accompanied by flourishes of her reddish hair.

Everybody was always thrilled at her arrival, except for the Doll. Moreover, my mother's coldness, the cause of which she stubbornly tried to hide, only increased as the days passed. Clearly Izmini irritated her. And when she saw the Doll becoming annoyed, she persisted. We were all sure that she meant no harm.

It all started over a perfume. This was so like the Doll: a matter of lavender water, as they called perfume in Gjirokastra.

I remember very well the day when what would later be called 'the incident of the German's perfume' took place. Three Germans had come to search for weapons. They turned everything upside down, including my grandmother's trunk and the Doll's hope chest.

Soon after they left, the Doll could be heard sobbing. They had taken her perfume. Her best and most expensive, which her father had ordered from Salonica on the day of her engagement.

The incident would be remembered for a long time. Izmini Kokobobo was the first to say, laughing, that for the Doll the whole of World War Two was summed up in that lost perfume.

The Doll was not noted for her argumentative skills, but nevertheless replied that of course she, Izmini Kokobobo, would say that, because she thought that her own lavender water ... like everything else of hers ... was the best.

My sister and I both thought that the senseless rivalry between these two women had started with this exchange at dinner.

In fact, there were even earlier signs of the

Doll's vanity and self-regard, so unlike her usual shadowy self-effacement. This was especially striking when we set off together to visit her father. According to a custom that the post-war new order had still not succeeded in abolishing, the city's women, when they 'went to their father's', were escorted by a Roma woman. This woman carried a bundle with a change of clothes, and the baby if there was a child, while the escorted lady carried only her parasol.

There were two such women living near us, Zëra and Vito, mother and daughter, who regularly accepted requests to act as escorts.

On the way to my grandfather's, the Doll maintained a theatrically stiff appearance. My uncles, chancing to meet her at the gate, responded to her in similar stage voices: 'Welcome, Mrs Kadare!'

When I reached the age of twelve, they thought that I too was infected by a touch of vanity.

It was 1947. The newspaper *The Young Penman* had made fun of me in its 'Replies from the Editor' on the fourth page, and to emphasise the mockery, had printed my name as I had written it myself: Ismail H. Kadare.

Worse luck, my two uncles had seen that reply, and almost in one voice said to me that if I had decided to follow in the tradition of swollen-headed Kadares, and call myself Ismail Hello Kadare, on the model of Lev Nikolayevich Tolstoy, I should henceforth insert the prefix *de*, as the French writer Balzac had done. According to them, having grown up plain Smajl Kadare I would end up as Ismail de Kadare, which meant nothing. They did not fail to point out that the name 'Ismail' did not at all suit a famous writer, although 'Kadare' had real class.

Two years later I was involved in an incident, which showed the disadvantages of fame. Together with a schoolmate, I ended up in prison. Not in the house prison, as some people thought at first, but in the real one, the state's. It was a tale of some counterfeit five-*lekë* coins, made of lead, which I had shown to all and sundry. They arrested us during our gym lesson and we slept for two nights among handcuffed prisoners. Although we had not broken the law, a trial was held according to the proper procedure. Our lawyer, Hilmi Dakli, took his place at our side. The presiding judge intoned the words 'In the name of the people'. My father stood there in the courtroom, just as he had done hundreds of times during his life as a court summoner. For him, it must have been like a bad dream. This was the second occasion that I had entered his own sphere: a short while before, as if to measure up to him, I had earned a fee, in actual money. And now I was in court. Soon I would be imitating him by asking, 'When will this house be repaired?'

When my uncles later found the notebook in which I had started my first novel, they told me that they were finally sure I suffered from megalomania. Three-quarters of the notebook was filled with advertisements along the lines of: 'The century's most demonic novel, hurry to the Gutenberg bookshop, buy I. H. de Kadare's magnificent posthumous novel,' with the price in gold *franga* and so on, whereas the text of the novel took up no more than five or six pages, and was incomplete, because, apparently worn out after the advertisements, I had abandoned the project.

When my first book of poetry was published and a telegram arrived from the publisher summoning me to Tirana, my father unexpectedly decided that I should go the whole way by taxi. It was this last bit, the taxi, that drew the most attention. Many people asked me in astonishment, 'Did you really go all the way to Tirana in a taxi?' Some people did not believe it, and others thought that going by taxi was part of publishing a book and becoming a famous writer.

6

AFTER ANY exciting incident, the house seemed even duller. That winter the wind whistled more loudly through the rafters, out of spite. For some time my grandmother had refused to come downstairs, supposedly because of the pain in her knees, although it was hard to tell when this was in fact out of spite and when it was not.

Nor did any real news come from my grandfather's house, except for the letter that my eldest uncle Qemal Dobi had sent from Budapest. He wrote that everyone was asking him if he was related to the president of Hungary, István Dobi.

I started two novels, one after another, driven more by impatience to use my ordinary name, Smajl, on the advice of my younger uncle, rather than any desire to write. So I left both unfinished, not even getting halfway through the advertisements.

In 1953 my grandmother died. Her departure ended what might be called 'the judicial era' in our house.

The sudden emptiness bewildered everyone, especially the Doll. I thought more than ever about her long-running irritation with my grandmother, and still I could not work out who had been in the right. Even today, after so many years, I cannot find the truth, and I even think that perhaps I have no right to look for it, as happens when the bitterness of a quarrel is so deep that any mere explanation pales beside it.

It was at about the time of my first book of poetry, or rather my taxi ride, when the Doll first asked me if I had really become *famous*, as they said, and then braced herself to ask something else. Boys like that, when they became so . . . that is, celebrated . . . did they take their mothers with them to where they went? It was a while before I worked out that she was talking about boys like me. Still, I couldn't understand her. 'Where should they take them?' I asked her. 'In the taxi? To the publisher?'

Finding it hard to explain, she got angry.

She came back to this conversation a few days later.

'Will you listen to me a bit?' she said. 'I want to have talks.'

For a while, she had been speaking in unusual phrases, like those of newspaper headlines or 'Microphone Theatre'.

'Talks,' I repeated to myself. Bilateral government talks.

'Don't laugh,' she said, 'I'm serious.'

Even though she had apparently long prepared for these 'talks', she made a mess of everything.

Finally, I grasped the gist of what she wanted to say. She had heard that boys, when they became *famous*, swapped their mothers.

Try as I might, I couldn't help laughing.

'What? What?' I repeated, interrupting her. 'They swap their mothers if they're unsuitable?'

'Don't laugh, Smajl.'

'You mean they choose a different mother, an opera singer for example? Or a member of the academy? Who told you such nonsense? Izmini Kokobobo?'

The Doll lowered her eyes.

I went on roaring with laughter, because I sensed that it was making her feel better. Slightly relieved, she too started to smile.

'But, Mother, how can you believe such nonsense? Are you really so silly?'

She went on smiling in her confusion, but didn't admit that it was her cousin from the capital who had given her this idea.

Izmini Kokobobo's next visit made it obvious.

The Doll could not conceal her apprehension. As on previous occasions, Izmini didn't avoid argument, and indeed provoked it further. 'What have you got against me?' she asked.

My father didn't usually care for loud laughter, but was untroubled by our cousin's. This seemed to upset the Doll. 'What have I got against you?' she blurted out bitterly. 'You think you're the bee's knees because you went to school in Italy. That's what I've got against you.'

This time, Izmini's mirth was so explosive it drowned out her own words and the Doll's replies. Then, in the middle of this exchange, something shifted. 'What?' said Izmini, and the Doll made no reply, which led the other woman to repeat in the ensuing silence, 'What?'

The Doll, as stubborn as ever, did not answer.

Izmini Kokobobo's expression froze. 'You mentioned Enver,' she said. 'Could you explain more clearly?'

Astonishingly, my father, who generally did

not interfere in such matters, interrupted. Later it struck me that perhaps the sudden creation of a courtroom atmosphere made him pipe up. 'You mentioned Enver Hoxha,' he said to the Doll. 'I thought you did too.'

The Doll must have said something sour, because Izmini Kokobobo's expression remained icy. The Doll was still silent and my father repeated: 'So what were you trying to say? Speak up, explain yourself.'

A long time later, I would remember the Doll's face in connection with what I had come to think of as the secret terror of white plaster, which the Doll would one day inspire.

The Doll's explanation was astonishing. 'I wanted to say that if she was as much a lady as she seems, Enver Hoxha would not have thrown her out because . . .'

'Because of what?' my father said. 'Speak up.'

After a short hesitation, the Doll replied, 'Because she didn't know how to make conversation.'

Izmini Kokobobo's face went pale.

'You don't know what you're talking about,' my father said to the Doll. 'Where did you hear such tittle-tattle?'

I waited for Izmini Kokobobo to say the same, but she remained silent.

My grandmother was no longer there to change the topic of conversation (mentioning somebody's rheumatism had been her favourite way of doing this), but although it took another direction of its own accord, everyone kept thinking of what had just been said.

The more I thought about it, the more illogical it all appeared to me, starting from the very idea of being thrown out for being a poor conversationalist. But Izmini Kokobobo's state of shock baffled me more than anything.

Although the Doll never told where she'd heard about it, this incident involving Enver Hoxha in Tirana was true. Izmini Kokobobo had been acquainted with the future chief a long time ago in

Gjirokastra, and in clandestine circles in the capital city. Later, after the establishment of communism, she sometimes went for lunch to the Hoxhas, until one day a careless remark put an end not only to her visits but to her entire career. It was a casual conversation, in which the party was mentioned, or more accurately the party's view of such-and-such an issue, when an expression had escaped her lips in the joking manner of former times: 'Oh, come on, what the party thinks – you mean what you yourself think . . .'

Enver Hoxha had frowned and said, in a serious voice, that Izmini Kokobobo had a mistaken idea of the role of the party. This was enough for the door of the first house in the country to be closed to her forever.

The year 1953 seemed extraordinary, or sometimes quite the opposite. Various events took place between the deaths of Stalin and my grandmother, but it was hard to predict whether they would be remembered or not. The most sensational of these was the arrival of condoms in the city pharmacy. There were contradictory instructions permitting and prohibiting them. It was suspected they might be a test to identify any weakening of the class struggle after the death of Stalin. But then it was realised that the measure was at the insistence of the Soviets and was linked to women's rights (Rosa Luxemburg, etc.), and after some hesitation by the party committee over whether communists should be advised to avoid the pharmacy and leave these bits of rubber to the increasingly depraved bourgeoisie, everything calmed down.

Our house remained desolate. Waiting for the publication of my book of poetry, I wrote some prose, and for the first time I did not fill most of the notebook with advertisements and self-praise. I stared in amazement at the first page on which I had written 'On Foreign Soil, October 1953'. There was nothing about a demonic or Dante-esque work, no encouragement to run to the bookshop, and especially no price in gold *franga* from the time of the monarchy.

Meanwhile, this business of publishing poetry seemed to me unreal. When somebody referred to it, I would remember the taxi journey, and not the book.

Surprisingly, this did not make me more modest. On the contrary. It was Ela Laboviti who first pointed it out: 'You've got very big-headed recently.' Then, a time-waster who never opened his mouth about anything said the same thing, and I dimly grasped what had happened. The advertisements and boasts that I had eliminated from my new prose-writing were determined to find a way out, and had found one. My conceit had been displaced.

The Doll had her own ways of knowing things, although more of taking no notice of things, and became aware of my swollen head. In her mind, fame and conceit appeared to be the same thing, and she mixed up these words in her own way.

When one day my cousin and loyal friend Bardhyl B. came to me with a black eye, I realised the Doll was not the only one who'd got confused. Bardhyl B. had been fighting with the boys of 3C over the very issue of my big-headedness.

The quarrel wasn't about whether I was conceited, because both sides agreed on this, but something else: did I or did I not have the right to be conceited? According to Bardhyl B., I had every reason: I published poems in the literary press, and received fees. I had travelled by taxi to take my book to Tirana, I had spent two nights in prison, and finally I had written two love letters to a girl in 2B.

The fight was over the last point: the love letters. My imprisonment was not considered to my credit, but a disgrace, especially because I had been defended by a bourgeois lawyer. But it was unclear whether I was a winner or a loser in the question of love. In fact, this was not very clear to either Bardhyl B., who took my side in all possible circumstances, or to myself. Bardhyl B. had passed the letters to Ylberja, our faithful friend, and because the girl in question had neither burst into tears nor threatened to hit me on the head with her shoe, but had on the contrary said 'thank you', we counted it a victory. But to our opponents the opposite seemed true, and moreover they said the two letters were wretched ones. They then recalled the case of a boy from the next neighbourhood, who came from the capital city and wrote one hundred and seven letters to a girl in his class, and was consequently excluded from every school in Albania.

As he talked, Bardhyl B. could not hide being slightly annoyed with me. At first I could not understand why, but then he came out with it. It was about removing the boastful advertisements, some of which we had assembled together. According to him, I could do what I wanted with literature – that was my business and he wasn't interfering – but where my fame was concerned . . .

I had obligations . . . at least . . . towards . . . my friends.

His words became confused, but from the movement of his head and his reddened cheeks I understood what he was driving at.

In fact, even though I tried not to show it, I felt guilty.

We came back often to this subject of big-headedness. Everyone spoke badly of it, especially in proverbs such as 'conceit is the vice of the clever', but this made no impression on us. Bardhyl B. and I made no secret that we thought the opposite. What was wrong with being big-headed? Why should it bother anyone? Bardhyl B. especially liked to enlarge on this latter point. Take your case for instance, he would say to me. Being big-headed makes you happy. Other people envy you, but you don't envy anybody. What business is it of other people if you think you're like Shakespeare? In the end, that's a matter between the two of you, Shakespeare and yourself. Particularly as he's long gone. So why should other people butt their noses in? Right?

I stared at him fixedly, and wondered how it was possible for this person to have exactly the same thoughts in his head as I did.

The question of big-headedness became more complicated when it was entangled with other issues such as poetry, money or prison. It was a knot that seemed impossible to untangle. You could make money from poetry, but if you made money yourself, you went to prison. Besides, it was said that poetry could send you to prison anyway. And as for conceit, the prevailing view was that it played a part in all of this. This idea was so wide-spread that the Doll asked me if they sent me money because I was big-headed!

I had recently noticed that everything was open to serious misunderstanding. Shortly before, my sister, whispering into my ear as if confiding a secret, told me that she was probably the daughter of our grandmother.

I put my finger to my temple to tell her she was crazy, but she replied that I didn't understand these things and then ran away in a rage.

I was sure that everyone was taking offence and ready to argue over the slightest thing. And when everyone was quarrelling, one could imagine the effect of all these quarrels on the Doll.

After her unexpected triumph over Izmini Kokobobo, she had become withdrawn again. One day, when she said with that uncertain expression that was now familiar to me that she wanted to have *talks* (talks between Vyacheslav Molotov and John Foster Dulles were being extended), I could again barely keep back my laughter.

As soon as she opened her mouth, I realised that it was once more the story of changing mothers, but this time in an even more dramatic light.

'Now that you're famous you're not thinking of renouncing me, are you?'

'What?' I said. 'This nonsense again? And for God's sake where did you find that word?'

She kept her eyes lowered and did not reply.

I insisted that she should at least tell me what she meant by that word, 'renounce'.

Finally she managed an answer.

'I wanted to say, to see the back of me.'

'Ah, you meant disown you. Now I understand.'

Again I wanted to laugh, but something restrained me.

She seemed to interpret my silence as hesitation, and so blurted out everything. 'I brought you into this world,' she sobbed. 'Let them say what they want. I am your mother, you don't have any other.'

Finally, I shouted, 'That's enough, Mother.' I asked her how she could be so silly, such a silly-head, and because I couldn't think of any other phrases beginning with 'silly', I ended, under my breath, with the word 'idiot'.

I was no doubt trying to say that Izmini Koko-bobo had been making fun of her again, but I remembered that she did not visit anymore and a wave of real anger swept over me.

She should at least tell me where she had heard such rubbish, or stop tormenting me with these things.

When I was about to say, once more, 'How can you be so silly . . . such an . . .' she uncharacteristically interrupted me:

'I am not an idiot.'

She had caught that word which I had always been careful never to say until now, and which I'd regretted as soon as I uttered it.

'I'm not an idiot . . .' If only she had said it in a stern and harsh tone, but her voice was low and gentle, almost ashamed. As if this were not already painful enough, she burst into tears. They were those familiar tears, as soft as in cartoon films, real doll's tears, and for this very reason harder to bear.

A pang of tenderness, sharper than ever before, stabbed me like a knife, and with it the thought that from then on I would be the source of her greatest and yet most absurd fear, that I would turn my back on her. Its absurdity did not render it any easier to allay.

How could I explain to her that there was not a shred of truth in all this? And that, even if there were boys who thought to exchange their own mothers for a more exquisite kind with fur coats who, like in the movies, played the piano at moments of sorrow, kept secret letters and other confidences (Mrs Kadare's mysterious Saturdays, for example), these were ephemeral fantasies, which in the realm of literature meant nothing. Our standards were different.

I knew that it was impossible to explain this, and still more impossible to tell her that not only did her limitations not hem me in, but as the years passed I had grown to appreciate these frailties as a sign of her superiority. I came to think that it was precisely from her skewed analysis of the appear-ances of the world, from this blurred and perverse reasoning, in short from this determination not to let go of the nature of a child, that what was called the 'writer's gift' was born.

I felt less the son of a mother than of a seventeen-year-old girl whose growth had been arrested.

It was not easy to get used to this idea, especially when I was growing up myself, approaching this age of seventeen at which she had remained. Incredibly, when I entered my twenties, she stubbornly remained seventeen. Eventually I became double her age.

This distortion of the course of time brought further turmoil in its wake. Sometimes I thought that all those things we say we learn at our mother's breast had come to me from another kind of milk, quite different from the Doll's. Lapses that seemed to me delightful, examples of back-to-front reasoning whose trail, once lost, can never be recovered, lodged themselves in my memory.

Schools, each more dangerous than the last the more complicated they became, insisted on trying to remedy these errors, to eliminate them, and free me from them, supposedly for my own good. But in fact they merely crushed me.

Meanwhile, together with the Doll's failings, and as a way of preserving them, I had sucked from her doll-like breast the very sense that I mentioned earlier, a cold terror like a carapace of white plaster, whose inhumanity would, it seemed, protect me from the fear of people.

Sometimes it seemed to me that everything that had harmed the Doll in life became useful to me in my art. Indeed I almost started to believe that she had accepted her own self-impairment in order to be useful to me.

She surrendered the freedom and authority of a mother – in short, turned herself into a doll – to give me all possible liberty as a human being, in a world where freedom was so rare and hard to find, like crusts of rationed bread in the time of the Germans, which she broke off from her own small portion and secretly gave to me.

It was impossible to untangle this knot.

Attempting to understand it more clearly, it has seemed to me, in those transcendent moments when you know one's insights will last no longer than an instant, that one must look for an explanation only above, in the highest spheres.

She would not have understood this in a thousand years, and would depart this world none the wiser.

Unknowingly, she had set herself up in a vain and tragic confrontation, with herself on one side and her son's so-called art on the other. One of the two would give way.

No doubt she knew that she had lost.

Her appeal – do not disown me – in fact meant: Disown me, if this helps you . . .

Had she invented that childish delusion herself, and blamed Izmini Kokobobo? Or perhaps it was something normal in her world . . . among dolls . . . this art–mother jealousy.

It seemed these two worlds would never come to an understanding.

At that faraway dinner in Paris, speaking Russian so that others would not understand, Voznesensky had tried to explain to me the inexplicable: his quarrel with his own mother, Russia.

Matma, Mamterr, Mater . . .

7

F OR SOME time the house had been sending
out signals, as if moved by a premonition of
its abandonment. Two of these signals, the creak-
ing rafters at night and the worsening leaks in the
roof, were very obvious. But there was no question
of any repairs.

My sister was the first to leave for the capital city,
with a scholarship. Then my grandmother left for
Vasiliko – 'the basil bed', as the city cemetery was
called, perhaps the only one in the entire Balkans
named after a flowering herb. Meanwhile my two

uncles had finished their studies abroad, one coming back with an ear missing and the other with a Russian bride. After the appearance of my book and a fruitless wait for an answer from the Gorky Institute in Moscow, I went to Tirana (by bus this time) to enrol, with a slight sense of injury, in the Faculty of Literature.

Bardhyl B. left shortly after me, because, as he wrote in his first and last letter to me, life in Gjirokastra had lost all meaning after my departure. We never met again, although I asked after him several times. They told me that he'd become a taxi driver in Vlora, and my guilty feeling that I may have inadvertently been the cause of this was assuaged by the soothing thought that between the two incidents of my early life, the mini prison sentence of two days and the taxi, he had chosen the latter as his model.

I did go to Moscow, and after my return, my parents moved to the capital city.

At first they were both disoriented, especially

the Doll. Her expression, 'the house eats you up', which she had used of the large house, now acquired an opposite meaning, because the small apartment ate her up worse than ever.

This was merely the beginning. After three weeks, we two sons of the family, that is myself and my brother, who had meanwhile entered the Faculty of Medicine, set off in a truck 'to fetch the things from the house'.

As if the exhausting journey were not bad enough, what awaited us at our house, the selection of the furniture and belongings we had to take, was a nightmare. Helped by two removal men, we started work but in a totally haphazard and illogical fashion. We were irritable, and remembered almost nothing of the many instructions not to forget this or that. We had a feeling that we were taking unnecessary things and leaving things we shouldn't, but there was nothing we could do. We broke the chandelier in the 'great drawing room' while trying to prise it loose, and our search of the Doll's hope chest was perhaps even more careless than when the German took the perfume in World War Two. The only things that were easy and indeed a pleasure to select were the carpets and rugs. The most awkward, not to say frankly resistant, were the copper utensils.

Surfeited with books in Tirana, I had decided to ignore any 'cultural heritage', but at the last moment I gave in and took from the chest containing my notebooks a handful of 'novels with advertisements', three or four plays, the manuscript of *Macbeth* and the only novella without advertisements, finally entitled *In an Unknown Land*.

The return journey was a particular nightmare. The further we left the city behind us, the more convinced we were of the mistakes we had surely made. The truck shook more and more. At the Këlcyra Gorge, the copper baklava tray fell out. As I dozed, I heard it clang as it fell into the ravine. The driver stopped the vehicle and we got out to look for it, but there was nothing we could do.

In fact, my brother, when he saw I had selected it, had asked me, 'What do we want this for?' I made no reply, but was thinking that perhaps we might need it at some future wedding. I had just got to know Helena, and my mind obscurely linked the tray for baklava, the symbolic wedding pastry, to the possibility of marrying her, and there and then, without giving any explanation, I had said to the baggage carrier, 'Take this!'

Its fall from the truck left me with an unpleasant presentiment. Shortly after, as I dozed again, I found myself talking to it: 'You didn't want to serve us . . .'

In my groggy state, it seems as if I thought that old tray, so loyal to the house, did not want to enter service outside it, and had decided it was better to hurl itself into an abyss than be used in this way.

How crazy, I thought drowsily. Such fancies were perhaps my last bond with the old house, from which I was now freeing myself.

When we arrived in Tirana towards midnight, instead of resting we were faced with the further chore of unloading the truck and carrying the furniture into the apartment. A more hellish experience could not be imagined. Some of the items would not fit through the door at all, and others got stuck and were cruelly crushed. Apart from the soft rugs, which huddled where they were thrown like frightened cats, everything else acquired a look of indignation. Alarming iron utensils, clothes props, oil lamps, copper or porcelain vases, all kinds of jugs and forks, seemed to howl as soon as you touched them. The apartment, as if violated by some monster, was full to bursting.

The Doll endured it as long as she could, and then put her hands to her head and broke into a wail. It was the first time I had seen her distressed over the old house.

The upheaval lasted for days on end, especially for the Doll and my father. For the rest of us, it made the events taking place outside the household seem much less dramatic. The quarrel with Moscow was getting worse every day. A break of diplomatic relations was expected, and after this, something that until recently would have astonished us more than the end of the world: war with the Soviet Union!

For a while, as if some pact of silence had been sealed, nobody mentioned the house. My father dealt with it. One day, after he came back from the café, he announced that the house had been rented out, as if this were a short news report. He said something about the number of tenants and, after a deep sigh of the kind he usually concluded with an 'eh!', added: 'Eh, tenants ... all with Greek names.'

I had learned in my student life in Moscow that a silence did not mean that the unmentioned had been forgotten.

There, enchanted by the big city, I'd been sure

that I had not only forgotten my old house but that the city of Gjirokastra, and even Tirana and the whole of Albania, had been erased from my memory for ever.

Something that in the writers' school was quite normal, but at the same time seemed to come from heaven, brought an unavoidable change into my life. The novel. The desire to write one was something between an order and a temptation. I knew that communism had founded this institute, at the very heart of its empire, not to cultivate literature but to destroy it. So I was a soldier of a death squad, summoned to do my pitiless duty of assault and slaughter.

However, even before recovering from the Pasternak scandal, in which some writers had badly disgraced themselves, more than half of the students had embarked on their novels. In the mornings, during the classes of what might be called the 'black mass', the lectures against the Joyce-Kafka-Proust trio, we learned that we must not write like them; while at nights, tortured by doubt, we could hardly resist the temptation of writing precisely in their manner.

This torture was their revenge. However, it seemed a blessed kind of payback.

In a last attempt to avoid these writers' accursed influence, I had decided to use a recently invented technique of not writing, but rather tape-recording. At least, Joyce and Proust had not known it, and certainly not Kafka. I felt somehow close to the latter, perhaps because our names began with K.

Most of the student writers of novels, as if fulfilling a promise, described the places where they had been born: the cities, villages, mountains, steppes, fjords, tundra or canyons. Nostalgia for these places was for some accompanied by a kind of superciliousness towards Moscow, the treacherous beauty who tried to employ her charms to estrange them from their birthplaces.

I was not a part of this clan, especially because I was sure that the girls of Moscow, though not those of the cloddish Soviet Union, were the sweetest in the world, an opinion I thought would never change.

So I was not a Moscow-sceptic but, without knowing why, I unexpectedly obeyed a call in the blood, remembered something that I was sure I'd forgotten forever: the city of my birth.

So you forgot me? But you remember me now I'm useful?

I was sure that I had no need of this city, and neither our professors nor dogma forced us to write about our home towns. This urge had no connection with the merits of these places, but with the recesses of our souls.

If I dared try to explain the inexplicable, I would say that if this city appeared to me grim and reproachful, like the ghost of a murdered king, this wasn't its fault but mine. Just as it wasn't to blame for its reputation for producing two kinds of people: the famous and the crazy.

This was a good opening phrase for a novel,

but I sensed that, like so many promising begin-
nings, it might be badly misinterpreted. The big
boss came from the same city, and this was enough.

The harder I tried to forget this phrase, the firmer
it stuck in my mind. It was a city that produced . . .
strange . . . people. A city that . . . how to put
it . . .

The beginning of an old song partly allayed my
doubts:

> *Renowned Gjirokastra*
> *Home of Shemo the thief.*

It wasn't clear to me who Shemo the thief was,
and still less whether he was mentioned for good
or ill. However, I thought of myself and imagined
the text should read, 'Home of Shemo the thief
and . . . me.'

This created an obscure parallel between myself
and the bandit of the song. It couldn't be said out
loud, but I was like him, if not worse than him, an

art murderer, a bandit of literature, who was even going to a college where elite troops were trained to learn how to kill better.

In the end, without delving deeper into my conscience, one cold Moscow evening I wrote on a sheet of white paper my name and then the word 'novel'.

Of course, I remembered the many openings of novels that I had written, or rather the advertisements for them, and with them Bardhyl B., who had been the author of some of them. After a little wave of nostalgia, as if to stress the stubborn fact that those times would never return, I felt the wish, after the word 'novel', to add 'without advertisements'. In other words, this novel, unlike the previous ones, would be without bragging and swank.

At the same time, my mind was subconsciously working on the title. I knew that the novel would be about a distant city that resembled neither Dublin nor Prague, nor Proust's Combray, and the idea of the 'city' wandered through my mind, a city with a few characteristics that made the place dull and lacking, mixed up with the word 'advertisement'. So it was a city that lacked something, like flowers or straight roads.

In this muddle, the word 'advertisement' suddenly shifted from describing the novel (a short novel, one without flowers or advertisements) to the city.

City Without Advertisements. I looked in astonishment at my title and I thought it was the stupidest title in the world, about illuminated advertisements, which did not exist in gloomy Gjirokastra, nor in Tirana or anywhere else in Albania.

I struck a line through the title, and with unnecessary haste looked for a new one. *City Without . . . City Without . . .* It had to be a city without something.

Finally, I thought I had found it. *City Without Taxis.* That's it, I said to myself. Even though not perfect, at least the title meant something. It was impossible to use taxis in Gjirokastra because of the city's steepness. Except . . .

I sensed that I could not play tricks on myself. I had pretended to have forgotten it, but the symbol of the taxi, like the advertisements, rose up straight from the grotesque mock-epic of my adolescence. The famous taxi journey over the book (which I no longer wanted to remember), Bardhyl B. and all the rest had caught up with me there in Moscow, just when I thought I had left them behind for ever.

I crossed out this new title with the taxis and wrote again the old one, *City Without Advertisements*.

My mind worked feverishly, and I thought I had found my answer on the very first page. Late in the evening, the Tirana–Gjirokastra bus was approaching the city . . . without advertisements. Among the drowsy passengers, a young boy called Gjon looked out at the view with a feeling of total boredom.

That's how I would start the novel *City Without Advertisements*. A novel without . . . I stared at the title for a while, as if trying to get used to it.

Meaning a city that lacked something . . . or someone who did.

My temples were beating again.

But this city is missing me, I almost cried aloud. So it's a city without . . . me.

Finally you've come to your senses, Bardhyl B. would have said to me reproachfully. The most important thing is always yourself.

The city without me, I thought. But soon there came a doubt. Was it or was it not without me?

With me . . . or without . . .

The two possibilities chased each other round my mind. With me, of course. Who else was that boy with the bored gaze? Or, as the great English master had taught us, my ghost?

I was returning to the city like a shadow of the kind I would certainly have become if I had not gone to Moscow. In short, I would experience a life which, although it was not my own, nevertheless might have been, and so I had an obligation to live through it, if only as a ghost.

After moving to Tirana, the Doll settled in, for good or ill, and it was my father who lost his bearings.

Leaving his home seemed to upset his equilibrium. The house had given him all his authority and now took it away, along with his title of 'the Great Repairer'.

He would emerge gloomily from his bedroom and return gloomily from the café after reading the newspapers.

His new friends in the café probably asked about me, as his old ones had done. Since that distant day when he had given me a thick ear because of using his name (an imitation of Lev Nikolayevich Tolstoy), he had never laid a hand on me, or even spoken harshly to me.

Old magazines dating back to the time of the monarchy insisted on the unavoidable enmity between father and son. The story of King Oedipus, which they told differently to the way we had heard it at school, attracted me more and more.

Under their influence, I began to think of my relations with my father as a strange kind of pact, a ceasefire in a war that had never been declared.

Besides the non-existence of this war, there was something else that did not fit in: my father's severe presence. As I mentioned several times in notes I made, not only did he not annoy me, but I rather liked him. Bardhyl B. had of course influenced my perspective. According to him, my father's grimness was altogether more attractive than the milk-and-honey sweetness of his own.

We had discussed this several times and more or less reached the conclusion that there was something in our reading that we had failed to understand. Either that the severity of my father's presence was not real, but imagined by ourselves, or that another factor came into the story: the ghost of Hamlet's father.

The magazines predicted that father-son hostility would sooner or later lead to a dramatic conflict. In the lectures against decadent writing in Moscow, it was claimed that this was something said by 'the other side', the bourgeoisie. If they said it, it became twice as attractive to us, and four times as attractive if it was attacked by 'our side', the socialists.

Rightly or not, the notion of a ceasefire, that is of waiting for a future battle, had taken root in my subconscious, as we had recently begun to call it. Especially now that my father had arrived in the capital city, stripped of his titles, in a cramped prison-like apartment. I was no longer a school-boy in short trousers but in possession of two diplomas, an author of books, who knew many things, including that file on Oedipus with its dark secret.

This feeling of hostility, whether real or imagined, naturally led me to think that my father would either alter or break the pact.

I calmly awaited developments. Indeed, one day I sensed that I was heading for a possible confrontation (superiority of forces, attack, final counter-attack, etc.), and that involuntarily I was acting out the Oedipus story, that is the father-son conflict.

When my chief at the editorial board of the magazine *Drita* showed me in secret a confidential bulletin of Western news dealing with Albania, adding that I could take it home but should be careful to burn it after reading, I immediately thought of my father. He would be better than anyone at not telling secrets and burning forbidden writings.

This publication was called the 'yellow bulletin', a reference to yellow literature, as all forbidden books were called, and it was distributed to senior editors to keep them informed about 'foreign anti-Albanian poison'.

One day, when my father seemed exceptionally troubled, I trusted in his confidence, showed him the bulletin and told him about the instruction to destroy it after reading.

I knew his appetite for newspapers and current events, but I had never before seen his moroseness change so totally into a mixture of gratitude and childish joy, as if I had presented him with a most precious gift.

In her memoirs, Helena has described the full ritual of forbidden reading, of locking yourself in your own room, burning the pages afterwards in the stove, the inspection of the ashes, and all the rest.

My father's entire life changed. He would wait impatiently at home for my arrival like a poor man expecting his monthly cheque, a patient longing for his medicine or an addict yearning for his drug.

I fully understood him, because it was no small thing for a long-standing follower of the press to read news that was so different. At the same time, according to the logic of my imagined conflict with him, I imagined the yellow bulletin as a secret weapon that had totally reversed the fortunes of the war between us.

By the same reasoning, I came to realise that with great effort, and with the aid of this secret weapon, the 'perverted' bulletin, I had defeated my opposite number and taken him prisoner.

Years later, I related this story to a close friend who had problems with his father's authoritarianism, and he told me half seriously that it was odds on that Freud, if he were alive today, would revise his theory.

In what I knew of Oedipus and Freud, it was the Sphinx that impressed me more than anything else, and I set less store by the prospect of parricide and still less by any attraction to my mother. The Doll's austere silhouette made her particularly unapproachable.

As the years passed I'd got used to Freud, as if learning the secret impotence of a tyrant (who may scare others, but is more scared of something himself.) In Moscow, Freud suddenly regained his lost authority in my eyes. So much mud was slung at him that I felt guilty of failing to appreciate him. Rarely did I not love someone I was given instructions to avoid. I tried to correct this tendency, but it was hard.

A rumour unexpectedly rescued me from this suffering.

Usually, the Muscovite slanders were exactly the same as Tirana's: these decadents were paranoid, immoral, syphilitic. But in Moscow a rumour circulated about Freud that was so different that my Latvian friend Jeronims Stulpans called it 'dissident gossip'. According to him, despite the official attitude to Freud, a secret memorandum of Stalin advised the use of his theories to break writers under interrogation. Anna Akhmatova also referred venomously to 'the malignant psychiatrist'. This caused a wave of hatred against Freud to spread throughout the Institute, which was very confusing for the spies.

At the very moment when I had lost hope, my father was fully acquitted of all Freud's charges against him.

8

DESPITE HER bewilderment in the first weeks, my impression was that the capital city suited the Doll. Her spirits perked up, she learned the streets and went looking for relatives.

I was sure that the naivety in her character, perhaps a result of her constricted life in the city of her girlhood, would lessen in Tirana.

After a time, I noticed that the very opposite was happening. Her naivety only increased.

For a while I wanted to believe that it was perhaps the big city itself that fostered illusions in someone like the Doll. In the end, I discovered that this was not the case, when she tried to conduct with me the most serious conversation in her life, about a proposed engagement.

Although considered slightly old-fashioned, it was still not entirely anachronistic for a mother to advise her son about his future bride.

When one day she said to me, in the old-time manner, that she wanted to have 'some talks', I at first laughed it off, as usual. But when I realised what it was about, my laughter hurt my ribs. It took a while before it sank in that my mother was thinking of a bride . . . for myself.

I could hardly believe my ears. Yet out of curiosity I cut my laughter short and waited for her candidate. The Doll's proposal was not merely disappointing, but beneath anything I might have expected. It would be impossible to find a more mistaken choice among a million mothers' suggestions. In short, I heard my dear, good mother, as described in hundreds of poems, suggest that I should become engaged to ... a semi-prostitute.

This is what had happened: One afternoon there knocked on the door of our apartment one of my acquaintances of what my friends and I called the 'pre-Hellenic' period, the time before my relationship with Helena. This acquaintance was one of those girls with very forward behaviour who mixed in intellectual circles and acted as models in artists' studios. I had got to know her one evening after dinner with an artist friend of mine, and indeed it was one of the rare cases in which, before I imagined a girl naked, I saw her thus on the wall of my friend's studio.

Our first words while dancing were about this picture. With a sugary and supposedly bashful smile, the girl, nodding towards one of the nudes, asked me, 'Do you like it?' She went on to ask whether I could imagine who it was, and I said unhesitatingly, despite the bad light, 'Isn't it you?' Smiling, she said that she had asked the artist to change the face a little, so she wouldn't be recognised . . .

She was very sweet, and it seemed her honeyed tones had instantly attracted the Doll: 'Good morning, ma'am, is this Smajl's apartment?'

The Doll was taken aback, but invited her in and was totally enchanted by the stranger.

I had never before heard her praise anyone so fervently. She had been dazzled not only by her appearance and manners, but by her Shkodra accent, which reminded the Doll of the time when she had lived there. Especially the word 'ma'am', which the girl repeated so frequently.

In the first silence that fell between us, the Doll gave me a guilty but appealing look, saying that I wasn't listening to her at all, but this girl, she thought, was perhaps . . . such a *polite* girl . . .

'Mother,' I interrupted. 'I understand what you're talking about.'

'But you aren't listening properly.'

'How can I listen,' I said. 'You're talking nonsense.'

'That's what you tell me about everything I say.'

My laughter suddenly evaporated. The only thing was not to make her cry.

I thought of saying: Listen, Mother, that girl is not what she seems to you. But the explanation would have been difficult. I had to find a simple, comprehensible way.

'Listen, Mother, that girl seems polite, but she's . . . how can I say it . . . a bit loose. Do you see what I mean?'

She seemed to understand this, but it made no particular impression on her.

With a feeling of injustice towards the 'girl', I used some qualifications that she perhaps didn't deserve. Impatiently, so that the Doll would understand, I listed the labels one after another, and the thought struck me that in Albanian we have an excess of epithets for this kind of woman, who is slightly 'loose'. It was as if those words had

been the first Latin, Celtic, Byzantine and Ottoman influences on our language. For some reason
Ottoman words seemed the most appropriate in
this case.

'Do you understand or not,' I bellowed. 'Do
you want me to marry a whore? Say something.
Would you like me to have a bride like that? Just
because she called you "ma'am" forty times in two
minutes?'

I wanted to add that she had been seduced by
that wretched word 'ma'am', but I was satisfied
that I had succeeded in stopping her tears and I
didn't distress her further.

In her memoirs, Helena has described her first
lunch at our house, which was also the first time
she met my parents.

I have never understood, not even now after so
many years, what made me say to Helena, after we
had spent the entire morning in my room, 'Why
don't you stay for lunch?'

'Lunch?' she said in surprise, 'Why? What for?'

We had been meeting for several weeks, but had never talked about such things as getting to know my parents. Helena knew my sister, I don't know how, and she had once bumped into my younger brother on the stairs.

'Why?' I echoed. I wanted to give her a pretext, but not finding one, I said, 'Just . . . for no reason . . .'

Without further ado I stood up and left the room to tell the Doll that my friend was staying for lunch.

'Who?' asked the Doll. 'That blonde girl?' She didn't say 'fair-haired', which was the usual expression in Gjirokastra, especially in the old houses, where fair hair was particularly valued, but used a word that had just come into fashion.

I took this as a sign that the Doll was taken with this girl, which proved that I was right in thinking that, if it came to achieving an understanding between Helena and my stubborn family, my main hope lay in her hair.

But it did not turn out this way. A kind of frostiness in the Doll's face hinted that she still nursed a kind of pique that her own untimely suggestion had not been considered, and it had no doubt occurred to her that Helena was the reason.

She said nothing, but merely asked if she should tell 'him', meaning my father.

'Of course,' I said. 'We'll all have lunch together.'

It was only noon, and there was still time for preparations before our usual lunchtime of two o'clock.

Helena did not conceal her nervousness. To raise her spirits, I told her some curious stories about the Kadares, some of them involving the Doll's simplicity. I mentioned the incident with the 'model', and half in jest added that, because the Doll had been so entranced by the word 'ma'am', she should try to use it herself.

Shortly before lunch, I went to assess the

situation. From my father's suit and the expression on his face I realised that he 'knew'. My brother whispered to me, 'Helena's coming?' and I nodded.

At two o'clock, I led the way into lunch, with Helena following. A lunch that Bardhyl B. would probably have called the biggest event in recent Albanian literary history, or something that recalled Jefferson's Declaration of Independence or the German *Sturm und Drang* movement that we had recently covered in Literature.

My father, with his severe expression at the head of the table, was as always on a 'war footing'. The Doll's manner was, as usual on such occasions, a mixture of reserve and disdain. My sister, for some reason I couldn't understand, seemed to behave in a slightly guilty manner. Only my brother was relaxed.

'Good afternoon, ma'am,' Helena said in a tentative voice.

I could hardly keep from laughing. The Doll did not hear, or pretended not to. I thought it was better if she hadn't heard, because Helena's voice would probably have sounded totally lifeless, compared to the tinkling, kittenish tones of that other girl.

As the Doll set down the final course, I thought I detected something familiar in her face. Thin-lipped. I almost said it out loud. A grandmother. Perhaps a mother-in-law . . .

At the table, it was nearly impossible to keep the conversation going. Apart from some ordinary exchanges between Helena and my brother, the usual student talk about changes to the faculty rules, the conversation was like some text pasted together with great effort.

'Didn't I tell you?' I whispered to Helena, next to me.

She nodded, and this reassured me.

It was the Kadares' usual incomprehension, about which I had spoken to her. But this time there was justification for the coldness. Questions could be read in everyone's eyes: Who is this girl, why is she here, and what does this lunch mean?

Now and then I glanced at the Doll, imagining how she felt.

Your heart bleeds for that other girl, I thought. I know it.

For a while I continued this imaginary conversation with the Doll. This girl here, Helena, is beautiful too, isn't she? The Doll couldn't say anything about her looks. Indeed, Helena was more beautiful than the other girl who had appealed to the Doll, and fair-haired, like the girls on stage that she liked.

I felt slightly puzzled. I wanted to say, there's no reason to look so blank. This is only a lunch, and above all this is only a girl. But she's the one I love, and this is our own business, not yours or anyone else's. Do you understand now?

The sudden irritation I had felt without any visible cause left me as quickly as it had come.

I was still confused, but now differently. Some

time had passed since the lunches and dinners at the big house 'back there'. The Doll was now in the role of her own mother-in-law. There was nothing left for me but to assume the role of my father, who had to redress justice when war broke out between the two women. Especially as he had now surrendered and lost the post of Grand Inquisitor . . . The cycle was coming full circle . . .

'What an exhausting lunch,' I said to Helena when we went back to my room. 'Perhaps it was a mistake to invite you.'

'No,' she said, in the same unsteady voice in which she had uttered the words 'Good afternoon, ma'am?'

If anyone had told me that this lunch, apparently so senseless, held a secret meaning, I would have laughed.

Questions were indeed asked. Who is this girl? Why is she here? What does this play-acting mean? Yet in fact nobody, especially not Helena or I, was hiding anything. This was true first of all because we were totally ingenuous. We had come to this lunch guilelessly, without any ulterior motive or covert plan.

Later, as if in an aberration, or as a result of a psychoanalytic reading, it occurred to us that, unconsciously, we may have been tempting first ourselves and then other people with the faint prospect of an engagement.

I increasingly thought that the absurd theatre of this lunch concealed an implicit future wedding, like those still-nameless rooms in the house in Gjirokastra, a 'maybe-wedding', to use a word modelled on those not-yet-rooms.

Unspoken congratulations that had no right to be uttered hovered in the air, like the glint of a pin in Helena's hair that sometimes caught the light and then vanished with a movement of her head – signs and portents of an engagement waiting to materialise.

9

WHENEVER WE mentioned this subject, we agreed that we would never follow any tradition, especially as Helena had already been through a farcical engagement. Increasingly we went out in public together, to cafés, the Writers' Club and other places, as well as restaurants, until only hotels were left, and all the signs were that they were also in store for us in the not-too-distant future.

I'd told Helena how on the 'decadence course' in Moscow I'd heard about the atmosphere of the *belle époque* and its famous courtesans who kept company with distinguished writers. She took pleasure in hearing about these things, to the point that when her family, during a row that Helena herself has described in her memoirs, tried to pin her down with the piercing question of whether she 'wanted to become his mistress', she had obstinately replied, 'Yes, that's what I want to be, his mistress!'

The febrile atmosphere that clung to us went back, we were sure, to that Sunday lunch.

Underlying this fever was a question that I had thought had gone out of fashion: engagement. I had been among those who scorned such a thing, and my lines of verse, 'I don't promise you engagement . . . with all its plans, and still less marriage, with its days of boredom like pyjamas', had put Helena off too, as she candidly admitted.

Now, as if in revenge, these lines were coming back to haunt us.

To me, people said, 'We saw you in the Café

Flora with that student of literature, are you getting engaged?' To Helena, 'We saw you at the theatre with that character back from Moscow. Congratulations.' Or worse: 'We heard you made up with your ex-fiancé. What a good thing. Congratulations.' We soon realised that a single engagement could not provoke so many rumours. In Helena's case, there were two engagements, one broken and one potential, that dogged her feet. As if this were not enough, a violinist at the Volga Restaurant said that he would smash his instrument because of H. G., not to mention two men of letters who were expected to do the same to their pens.

Our resentment of the idea of engagement grew, and our desire to trample on tradition led us to the idea of vaulting it entirely and going straight to the next stage . . . marr . . . iage . . .

But I had also spared no criticism of marriage. People were right to ask me, what about all that defiance of pyjamas with boring stripes, and so on?

However, there was no going back for us. We could try to continue as we were ('Will you be his mistress?') or we could bow our heads and go straight to . . . to . . . what the hell could we call it . . . a union of matrimony . . . The phrase was reminiscent of Tirana City Hall, which it was said would soon break with the Soviet Union, itself on the brink of collapse. So to a kind of union . . . not the sort of marriage other people imagined, no way, but another kind, the sort that we wanted . . .

In truth, it wasn't clear to us what we wanted. An 'as-if' marriage *sui generis*, something that was and wasn't . . . In other words, a 'sort-of' . . .

As if to convince ourselves of our own determination, and so that nobody could think we were building castles in the air, we heedlessly set a date for the sort-of: 23rd October.

So it was no longer a matter of poetical flights or broken violins, but of a precise date for our union, at the proper time and place stated on the invitation.

Our announcement of 23rd October made both our families furious. Why this date and this sudden hurry? Why hadn't we threshed the matter out between the two parties? And where did this 23rd October come from?

We had selected the date at random. It had no secret or symbolic meaning, nor was it even convenient for Helena's final exams.

But nobody believed this. Our families thought only of whatever it might conceal, and each clan was sure that the other side knew what they themselves didn't, until one day Helena's mother arrived with a pale face at the girls' dormitory to ask frankly if the reason was not the unspeakable one . . .

After all these doubts were dispelled, it seemed likely that a 'constructive outlook', as the recent phrase for a positive attitude went, would prevail. But this did not happen. Just when the two families were preparing for a rapprochement, we two, Helena and myself, became uneasy.

Our anxiety was about the promise of a modern marriage that we had been announcing proudly everywhere: in cafés, in after-dinner conversations with friends and in my books. (As if one book in Albanian were not enough, a second had now come out in Moscow, translated into Russian by no less than David Samoylov, who was not only Jewish, but was rumoured to have been semi-engaged to the 'princess', as people referred under their breaths to Stalin's daughter . . .)

So we had to keep our promise that we would be . . . *marr* . . . *ied* . . . differently. Was this mere talk?

For the first time I became aware of what it meant to come up against a myth that was more than two thousand years old. Of course, we could act it out, but there was an alternative myth, equally ancient, if not older than this rite itself: abduction.

Astonishingly, in this country where nothing was allowed, there had been an unprecedented

wave of abductions, especially among the cooperative farms. Kidnapped brides, who were really
women engaged without their families' agreement,
were turning up everywhere. In short, abduction,
which lay at the root of the marriage rite, had
become comical and was no longer considered a
scandal.

The bride. The Nibelungs. Marriage with a dead
man. I tried to put these myths out of my mind
and almost regretted how I had scoffed at virginity, not to mention other things.

Time was passing. Helena and I had finally
agreed, first of all, to exclude our families from
the 'event', and replace both sides with her friends
from the faculty and 'my' writers and artists.

Helena's friends were amazed at the news.

I felt the absence of Bardhyl B., who would
have put the event in a global perspective, comparing it to a new future for Europe or something
similar.

I didn't find it hard to make our arrangements known at home. The Doll listened in total bewilderment, without uttering a word, apparently waiting for my father to announce his surprise or opposition, and unaware that the latter was still under the sway of the yellow bulletin.

Helena had still not mentioned anything to the Gushi family, but her silence had deepened their suspicions. Rumours circulated about an imminent scandal. Because her family no longer hoped for any response from Helena, her father was said to have taken it upon himself to solve the mystery. He found out where my father drank his morning coffee, put on his best suit and, discovering my father alone at a table, extended to him a visiting card left over from the time of the monarchy, with the words 'Dr Pavli Gushi, pharmacist'.

The conversation was difficult, especially at first. Not only was Helena's father sensitive by nature, but he did not find it easy to explain a situation that became twice as hard to resolve before my father's inscrutable stare.

He started very cautiously: There was no question of interfering, especially as they were young . . . but because of this . . . their fate . . . perhaps . . . although both sides . . . as you might say . . . we parents . . . our duty . . .

When he realised that the man opposite him did not understand, or was pretending not to, he changed his approach. Perhaps you know that your son and my daughter . . .

One can well believe (and he himself confessed as much afterwards) how having heard something of my father's character he waited fearfully for a rebuff along the lines of: I don't know anything about this. I don't go into these things.

But amazingly the reply was totally different.

'I know.'

Later we analysed their conversation blow by blow and agreed that the moment when my father pronounced the words 'I know' must have been decisive in not bringing this conversation to a sudden end.

What really happened between them?

Probably each had expected from the other bitter remarks like: 'Stop your son bothering my daughter,' or, 'Doctor, you would do well to convince your daughter, and then come to me,' and so on. But the magic phrase 'I know' had been uttered, and this banished any harsh words and even thoughts along the lines of: This man shows me his doctor's degree, but he doesn't know that I read the yellow bulletin, which is like reading the thoughts of the devil.

My father's 'I know' was deeper than any ordinary knowledge, because it acknowledged that Sunday lunch. This lunch was linked to the whole mystique of sharing bread at table, of eating together, something which goes far beyond eating, involving the most elevated conception and sworn covenant of the protection of a guest.

Helena had eaten bread in our house, and so, obscurely and irrationally, had created a profound connection with the Kadares, arising out of unknown regions.

Inadvertently, Helena had acquired a prerogative, that of a guest before that of a bride.

Encouraged by the breaking of the ice, Dr Gushi became persuaded of the goodwill of the Kadares quicker than he should have been.

Following an impulse of joy, after the not-very-explicit statement that 'seeing as this is how matters stand, they should think about everything together', he started talking about announcing the engagement, preparations, dowry, ring and so forth.

After each of these words, my father's face darkened as if he were hearing disastrous news. The doctor noticed this too late. He tried to repair the situation, but it was impossible. The harsh words expected at the beginning of the conversation were uttered at the end: 'I don't deal with these things. Talk to my son.'

The meeting, the first and last, had ended in total misunderstanding.

Meanwhile the facts collected by a branch of Helena's family were not promising. Dr Gushi had been naive to think that he could come to an agreement with the groom's family.

The Kadares all had a screw loose, everyone knew that. Who had ever heard of a father borrowing money from his twelve-year-old son? And the son going to prison two years later? And running away from home by taxi? And becoming a poet, trying to publish a book with a poem entitled 'Down with Virginity', as if virginity were American imperialism?

'It's up to you. But there's nothing you can do, if the girl won't be persuaded, leave this business in God's hands.'

*

The situation in our family was entirely different. It was a mixture of vain nostalgia and a kind of philosophical approach that involved remorse and pangs of conscience over the abandoned house in Gjirokastra. The house was almost three hundred years old, and so few weddings had been held in it, while this callow apartment, not even two years old, was in a hurry to host a wedding even before the plaster was dry (with the milk still wet on its lips, as you might say).

From the anthropological point of view (as it would later become the custom to say), this remorse was justified. The most recent weddings remembered in the big house were those of my grandmother and the Doll, in 1895 and 1933. None since then.

Then the family remembered the people who would not be coming to the wedding, the Doll's father, and my grandmother and her inseparable sister Nesibe Karagjozi, who had recently died. Two or three times, especially when it came to the subject of the big wedding cake (to be ordered from the NTLUS, an acronym whose expansion roughly meant the 'Socialist Pastry Cooks' Catering Enterprise'), the big baklava tray was mentioned, but softly and gently, as if it were an old lady who had died in not-very-clear circumstances.

10

THE WEDDING, in spite of every prediction, was held on 23rd October.

I already knew that at the heart of every wedding lay anger, which would inevitably burst out before, during or after the ceremony.

At our wedding, the hour of anger struck in the third act, immediately after the end of the ritual. It took the shape of an almighty quarrel between the two clans.

The vexation and resentment came from the most unexpected directions, and was expressed in the strangest ways, from quotations of Engels to Icelandic proverbs. 'We thought that the Kadares, once they got out of Lunatics' Lane, would recover their senses, but the opposite has happened, they're totally out of their minds.' 'Leave the Kadares alone, what about the doctor, why is he looking so woebegone? It's true what they say . . .' (and here followed some Latin or Mongolian proverb).

I felt that this malice had also infected myself, a sort of revenge for our disdain for tradition. 'That mother of yours shouldn't be seen crying in public on the train, heartbroken because her son-in-law won't call her "Mama" . . .'

This barb left Helena open-mouthed.

They were the first harsh words we exchanged after the wedding . . .

'My mother, crying on the train . . .' she repeated in a low voice, not taking her eyes off me.

It felt like an epilogue, like the end of a war, when each side tries to take stock of its losses. There was a sense that 23rd October would enter the annals of weddingology, as a 'failed attempt to achieve epic status'. I seriously missed Bardhyl B., the only person who would have been able to compose a commemorative text in its honour.

Most of the Kadares were dead, and thus cruelly indifferent. They used this ascendency as they had done thirty years before when they conquered the appalling Dobis. They made light work of crushing the Gushi clan. Nor did the latter's attempts at talks, or the diplomas of the city's most famous doctor and pharmacist, help in the least; it was as if Germany, having defeated Poland and France, were to hurl itself blindly against Switzerland.

Shortly after this we exchanged the large flat for two small ones opposite each other in the centre of Tirana. For the Doll, this cushioned the shock of the division of the household. But her relief was really due to something else: there had finally been a swap, but of apartments rather than mothers.

There was a vivacious atmosphere in both

apartments. Friends, mainly writers and artists, came to help put everything in order, and brought with them their own friends, who brought others in their wake.

Most were students who had returned from abroad after the big break-up had interrupted their studies. They were attractive characters in every way, with their energy, humour, and even their anxieties over foreign fiancées who had either remained behind in Albania and could not return to their own countries, or wanted to come to Albania and were not allowed to.

Artists tried out their colours on the kitchen shelves, using particular shades which, although never explicitly banned, were semi-forbidden. Others sorted out the library and the bedroom, teasing Helena by the by.

We were so absorbed in all this that we rarely gave a thought to what was happening outside. An extraordinary tension could be felt everywhere. If you turned on the radio, you quickly turned it off. The yellow bulletin, the family's secret watch-dog, was turning increasingly fierce.

My father was conspicuously absent from the upheaval. It was a real mystery how he managed to go out, come home and shut himself up in his own room without anyone noticing. Meanwhile I had never seen the Doll so animated. She drank coffee incessantly, darted from one apartment to the other, and was obviously happy to be at the centre of attention. ('Hey, Ism's mother, do you like this colour? Does the washing machine go here? Am I being a nuisance? Sorry, what did you say, Mrs Kadare?')

One day I saw her in the distance, her hand held by someone whose face was familiar. Soon I heard the girl's voice: 'Smajl, I'm so pleased to meet Mrs Kadare again.'

She drew her by the hand towards me, while the Doll kept her eyes lowered, as always when she felt guilty.

'Mrs Kadare is so delightful. We do enjoy chatting.'

'I know,' I said. The Doll lifted her eyes, perhaps to see if I was still angry.

I was no longer angry in the least, but I felt a sudden, familiar qualm at having spoken ill of the girl. Apparently she had come with one of the artists in the role of his assistant, either as a model or a lover, as happened with these girls who were cruelly called 'handy' (probably because they were passed from hand to hand), but who might be thought of as more fortunate than others, because after all they were in the hands of artists and poets, who put them on canvas or into poems before touching their bodies.

I had neither the time nor the opportunity to express my feelings, except by doing something that I did not do often: I stretched out my hand to touch the Doll's hair with the tenderness that a woman and her hair arouse at such sweet moments.

The Doll became even more enterprising. One day I found her listening with great attention to Pirro Mani. I was very curious to know what the

Doll could find to talk about with the most fashionable theatre director in Tirana. He was showing her a sheet of paper, while intoning in his booming voice: 'Ism's mother, this show will shake the whole of Tirana! Look, here are the two levels of the stage, one inside the belly of the monster, that is the wooden horse, and the other, at its feet, where Laocoön is arguing with the crowd.'

I realised that he was explaining his plans to stage my novel *The Monster*, whose still-unpublished manuscript I had given to him.

'Do you see now, Ism's mother. It will be a superb confrontation . . . Ah, here is Ism . . . I was explaining our next production to your mother. She has a special *feeling* for the theatre, have you noticed?'

'Yes, you might say so,' I said, and then turned to the Doll, to ask if she had understood.

At first she avoided replying, but when I pressed her, she muttered, 'Yes, that argument . . . that's what people are like these days, always quarrelling . . .'

I described this incident a little later to a small circle of friends. The Doll pretended not to hear, as if we weren't talking about her. Somebody said that the conversation would have gone better in the hands of Dritëro Agolli, who was well known for being able to talk to old people. My brother objected. According to him, the harder the conversation was to understand, the more it appealed to her. The Doll still pretended not to hear.

Some time later, another director, this time of films, told me one day, 'I know your mother,' and my brother who happened to be there burst out: 'What did you make of each other!'

Kujtim Çashku was famous for overusing foreign words. He had met the Doll on the benches of the Park of Youth, alongside the main boulevard, where she used to sit, sometimes with her sisters, sometimes by herself, 'to watch the world go by'.

As Çashku told me, the Doll was attracted not just by the theatre but by the view of the Hotel Dajti opposite, especially on the days when there were official receptions, stylish cars, foreign ladies getting out of them . . . what you might call all that *glamour* . . .

The Doll's taste for elegance and for drawing attention, such as I dimly remembered from the time when our little cortège, escorted by Vito the Roma, passed through Gjirokastra on the way to my grandfather's house, was apparently returning.

Her theatrical side probably responded to the appeal of the chic, a taste so long suppressed in her, probably since the German's theft of the perfume. She no doubt liked the dimension of secrecy (Mrs Kadare's mysterious Thursdays) that her plaster-like carapace encouraged.

On fine days, telling nobody, she would put on her best clothes and set off with her light-footed gait towards the main boulevard.

On rainy days, she had another destination, which we would perhaps never have discovered if a woman friend had not told us that she had come across the Doll quite by chance sitting in an armchair in the great lobby of the Dajti, watching people go up and down the stairs to the library and the big café on the first floor.

Asked if she were expecting anyone, she had said no, she was just 'giving her eyes a treat', an expression that our friend had never heard and couldn't understand.

I didn't find out anything else. In particular, I never discovered whether or not she went secretly to the theatre, although I suspected it.

Her panoramic view would include the arcade of Luigj Gurakuqi Street, the Palace of Culture, the Clock Tower Café where my father drank his morning coffee and from where the Doll surely wouldn't want to be seen, and then the National Theatre and Writers' Club, from where she would also not want me to see her, and then the Art Gallery and finally the Hotel Dajti itself. This was the map of her beau monde through which she moved, as if escorted by an unidentified companion, whether my father, me, all of us, or perhaps her alter ego.

II

WE KNEW that my father's end was close. He was still slim and straight, but one could sense death in the way he walked. It is significant that funeral marches move at a slow pace, as if to show that death is, among other things, a matter of rhythm.

Only at this pace could he descend beneath the earth, where the Kadares seem to be stronger.

When I reflected on this later, I thought of Pythagoras and the power of what is not yet incarnate. I seemed to have grasped something of it, but the wings that I imagined were giving flight to my thoughts suddenly failed me.

I had pitilessly mocked my non-existent novels, the ones with advertisements, and in Moscow I had even owned up to them in seminars on the psychology of creativity, reducing my friends on the course to helpless laughter. It did not occur to me that these books, just as they were, disembodied and shapeless, had an advantage: they were untouchable. They were in no danger from anything.

As we talked about the superiority of unwritten literature, with the usual hilarity, our professor interrupted to say that there had been child composers, but nobody could write literature at the age of twelve, or even fourteen.

This caused me a little pang to the heart. I had wanted to believe a while longer in the qualities of unwritten literature. After all, it was thanks to these non-existent books that I achieved that dream-like freedom not to be found anywhere else. They had made me believe that my enchantment with *Macbeth*, written by some Englishman called Shakespeare, gave me a special affinity to him, as to no one else.

My awe of Shakespeare did not lessen but grew to the point where I began to copy out the text. When I began to lose my temper with him, as I had done with Bardhyl B., I persuaded myself that I was not just close to Shakespeare, but almost a cousin.

I told B. B. this and had seldom seen him moved so deeply.

This ability to lose my temper with the Englishman struck both of us as the most convincing proof that I had become fused with him.

'Fused,' Bardhyl B. echoed, in a voice that I had never heard before.

I even thought that when I was a little more grown up – in other words, when I became clever – I would correct Shakespeare's mistakes, as far as I could.

I would start with the scene in which the ghost

of Hamlet's father appears. I was convinced that if Hamlet had been the son of my own father, he would not have behaved so carelessly during the conversation. It wasn't a question of respect, more a matter of not spoiling the beauty of the fear . . . For example, if my own father's ghost appeared to tell me, say, that the Doll's brothers, my two uncles, had murdered him in his sleep, both I and my friend Horatio – in other words you, Bardhyl B. – would speak rather differently . . .

At this point Bardhyl B. broke down entirely from emotion. We fixed our eyes on one another, and I awaited the fatal words: 'So why don't you start now?'

A short time before, something had happened that we didn't want to remember. In my feverish desire to write works of a kind never seen before, I had started my novel *This Is Victory*, which, in order to show that I was original and not to be compared to anybody else, I had started back to front, from the end.

Bardhyl B. and I were in my house, he in the room between two storeys that we considered belonged to the two of us, and myself in the drawing room where I usually wrote. It was afternoon, hot, and in the adjacent room my father was taking his nap. I finished and was about to descend the stairs, holding in my hand the page I'd written, that is, the end of the novel: 'The sun shone on the glowing fields of the cooperative and the villagers listened with happy faces to the partisan commissar who pointed to the meadow and said, "This is victory."'

The stairs creaked under my feet. My head was numb from exhaustion. Bardhyl B.'s stare was still more glazed.

'Did you do it?' he asked.

'What?'

'That mur . . .' (der.)

I nodded.

'You've gone pale.'

How could I not be, I thought.

I held the page of writing out to him.

Thou canst not say I did it.

I heard a knocking at the gate.

We both shivered.

'My father might wake up,' I said softly.

Wake Duncan . . . wake my father . . .

Bardhyl B. started reading the manuscript. He couldn't believe his eyes.

'I don't know what to say,' I said. 'I was thinking of one thing and something else came out.'

The page shook as he returned it to me. So did my hand as I took it from him.

The knock came again.

'I've got no words . . .' I said, almost sobbing.

I felt that I was rambling. No language could describe what I felt in my heart. I needed a different one. The one I had would not obey me . . .

This was perhaps the moment when I discovered the power of the unspoken.

For days on end, as if to convince myself how incomparably better it was not to communicate, we both, obscurely and irrationally, repeated the same thing, that we had no words.

A few days later he came to me and announced in one breath, as he usually did when bringing news, that he had read a novella in which there was another world or planet, that, although containing the same human species as ourselves, honoured as its greatest poet not Homer, as we do, but a tailor who had never written a single line.

I was about to say that this was crazy, but he forestalled me by saying that this might seem nonsense, but if you looked carefully at this story, it had to do with us . . .

It took a while for it to sink in that in this other world where everything was different, the important thing was not what you wrote, but what you *could* write . . . In other words . . .

In other words, it was the same in our case . . . with the novels that nobody knew about . . .

The terrifying novels that do not exist, I thought with a certain pride.

'And Homer?' I asked after a moment. 'The real one, ours, did he exist there, or had they done away with him?'

'He existed. In eleventh place, if I remember right.'

'The real Homer?'

'None other. With the *Iliad* and all the rest, the Cyclops, Helen of Troy.'

Fearing bad news, I didn't dare ask about Shakespeare.

When Bardhyl B., as if realising what was on my mind, uttered the words 'Whereas our William, he . . .' my heart skipped a beat.

'What?' I asked in a faint voice.

'The place of the world's finest dramatist had been usurped by an idiot who not only hadn't written a single play, but couldn't even read or write . . . So William barely hung on to seventh place.'

I consoled myself that maybe that wasn't too bad. However, Bardhyl B. uttered a 'but' that stopped my heart again.

'But William was up against another problem. They accepted his plays, but there was some doubt about whether he himself existed.'

For a while we strove amidst our bewilderment to work out which would be worse, losing the plays or the man himself.

I was totally confused.

'And who wrote this wretched story?' I asked with assumed indifference.

'Someone called Mark,' said Bardhyl B. 'Mark... Twain or something.'

We felt that we should be tearing this man to shreds, but we didn't have the heart. The fantasy of this Mark from America was somehow close to the miracle that we had long been looking for, a masterpiece that acquired its power from being unwritten.

Bardhyl B. thought that it was rather like the case of my own novels, of which only the advertisements were visible, while they themselves still lay underground. It was not for nothing that we liked to call them 'demonic' – that is, invisible, unseen. Isn't this the most common phrase for something that inspires awe?

Our intoxicated minds raced back to Shakespeare. His situation, apparently so different, resembled ours.

We tried to take the question calmly: Here was Shakespeare, and there were his plays. The world seemed not to have room for both. We had to choose between the man and his work.

My head swam again. We felt we hadn't quite hit the mark, although we'd come close. Famous yourself, but without your plays . . . or fame for your plays, but not for you . . . As you might say, life without fame or fame without life.

At last we seemed to be solving the riddle. In any event, we shouldn't break our ties with the netherworld, because it was only there that certain things not allowed in this world were permissible.

My novels had been a mistake, because they had

been born at a time when literature was forbidden. Like alcohol prohibited to adolescents. So they would remain deep down below, lying in rows, frozen between thinking and writing, and invisible to the human eye. I was sure that if any one of them stirred itself to be written, it would be annihilated at once, as if struck by lightning.

In the days after my father went to that next world which he may have considered his more natural home, my memories of Bardhyl B. crowded in as never before.

What's he doing? I wondered whenever he came to mind. Why don't I see him?

On my wedding day of 23rd October I'd had several premonitions that he would come in his taxi (his taxi playing the role of an old nag). Come so I can send you to abduct Helen, or whatever you like, as in the past, when everything was permitted to us.

At my father's burial, I reflected that, as the

saying goes, a friend may fail to come for joy but not for sorrow. He should have been present with his taxi down there on the road, ready to take my father to the proper place.

It would be no wonder if he came one day to take me . . .

Why wasn't he here? I had sent word again to Vlora, but in vain. Was he ill, I wondered . . . or worse, no longer in this world?

It was not for the first time this suspicion had occurred to me. I would have heard something unless . . . unless he had never belonged to this world.

I was stunned for a moment and shook my head as if to banish this terrible thought. But it would not go away. On my last visit to Gjirokastra, as I was climbing Lunatics' Lane together with an architect friend, my feet had instinctively stopped at the third gate on the left that must have been Bardhyl B.'s, but strangely it did not resemble his gate at all. The architect who was with me wanted to open it, but in a voice that seemed not my own, I cried, 'No.'

After my father was buried, the Doll retreated totally into herself. It took time for the apartment to regain its equilibrium. One evening, during an after-dinner conversation, a friend remarked that old houses preserved the memory of the dead for a long time, but modern apartments with their simple, smooth lines were designed to note a departure as casually as possible.

I remembered everything connected with him. People said contradictory things: some had found him formidable, while others insisted on his unusual sense of humour. Then both sides would turn their heads to me, to hear the truth.

Any explanation seemed impossible, especially when the conversation touched on father-son relationships, however obliquely. Perhaps the only secret I learned from him was how difficult it is to understand whether tyranny is a real thing or something one projects oneself. The same goes for enslavement. In the end, one can be the slave of a tyrant, but he is just as much your slave.

I calmly learned to search my conscience. My sister Kaku's engagement and then my younger brother's marriage both took place quietly. On the latter occasion, as expected, when it came to the cake I recalled the big baklava tray, and my suspicion of a crime committed long ago, that night at the Këlcyra Gorge. Did my brother really not see anything, as he dozed wrapped in rugs on the flat-bed of the truck, or did he notice that the old tray was about to fall off, and do nothing to prevent it?

People also began again to tease me about the Doll. Would I take her with me to Paris when my book was published there? Another version was more wounding: would I take Helena's aunt instead?

The girls in the house laughed, and the Doll tried to laugh too. Laughter seemed to relieve her more and more.

That was the last time the Doll laughed on this earth.

Anybody hearing those words will think first of death.

But the truth was even more galling.

Just before dusk on 24th October 1990, the phone rang and an unknown voice said: 'Listen to the radio!'

The news of my flight with Helena from Albania was being broadcast. A letter sent to the country's president. A call for free elections. The state's response was to declare me a traitor.

The Doll and Kaku were alone. They were staying in our apartment on Dibra Street, as usual when we were away from Albania.

They were stupefied. They trembled in the darkness, which gradually became more intense. They did not dare open the windows. The telephone rang again, but there was no voice on the other end. A little later, they lifted the receiver once more and discovered the line had been cut. As if finding only one thing to do, they started to weep, sometimes together, sometimes in turn.

After a while there was knocking at the door.

Two men entered first, followed by two more carrying metal chests.

The Doll did not remember the word 'search' being mentioned. Nor did my sister.

One of the men, a diminutive, gloomy character, stood at the entrance to the study. The other went up to our two bookcases.

From a distance, the Doll could hear them talking to Kaku.

'What did they say?' she asked when Kaku came past her, but my sister did not reply.

The raiders opened the glass doors of the first bookcase. The Doll couldn't believe her eyes. They were taking out the files of my manuscripts! She had imagined anything except what was happening before her. She told me later that she thought they might take her away in handcuffs, but not that they would touch these manuscripts. When I asked her why she thought this, she couldn't say. It seemed she believed these manuscripts possessed a secret power from having absorbed my thoughts over many years. Now, their magic spell broken, they were being passed roughly from hand to hand and thrust into metal chests.

'But didn't you think that when they left the apartment, the danger would disappear with them?'

'I don't know,' she replied. 'Perhaps . . .'

Her eyes assumed the expression they wore whenever she felt ashamed at not understanding something, a habit that some people called a failing and others a gift.

The chests were now being closed. The diminutive man, who was apparently in charge, supervised everything.

It was hard to figure out what was happening. It seemed to be the manuscripts that were causing confusion. The men circled round them in an ungainly dance.

The Doll was unable to make sense of the chaos. As if in a dream, she went up to the glum-faced supervisor, and asked him, 'Are you the person who will put me in prison?'

The man gave her a strange look.

'I am a prosecutor,' he said in a low voice, 'But don't be scared, granny.'

The uncertainty continued, and the foul taste of a nightmare spread everywhere. From our bedroom, Kaku emerged holding a revolver, like in the movies. The Doll thought that she would shoot, and cried out, 'What are you doing, you wretched woman?'

One of the prosecutor's men calmly took the revolver from her hand and looked at it carefully.

'This isn't the gun we knew about,' he said. 'This is unauthorised. Find the other one, that has a permit.'

Kaku opened her eyes wide, at a loss.

'Don't you put me in prison. I'm ill,' the Doll said to the prosecutor. 'My eyes aren't too good either.'

The prosecutor replied with the same words as before, in the same sad voice. Kaku returned with another revolver in her hand and the Doll would have said again, 'What are you doing, you wretched woman?', if one of the men hadn't calmly taken the gun from her. 'It was in the white bookcase,' Kaku explained. 'Behind De Rada's *Complete Works*. I saw it when I was dusting.'

The prosecutor's man examined it for a moment, and said, 'This is the one.'

The metal crates were full at last, and they carried them downstairs in silence. The melancholy prosecutor followed them out. By the door, he put his arm round the Doll's shoulders, and whispered in her ear, 'Don't cry, granny.'

I could not get this picture out of my mind. For years, my thoughts kept returning to that grief-stricken apartment on Dibra Street, where the two women, now left alone, burst into loud sobs as if in mourning.

12

WHEN I returned to Tirana for the first time in March 1992, of all the memories that came to me on the plane, that one had been the hardest to bear. Now the Doll sat silent on the settee, while a correspondent of French television filmed her. 'Cheer up,' everybody said to her. 'Let bygones be bygones.'

She did her best to smile, but evidently couldn't. Her eyes were haunted by that same guilty expression she wore when she did not comprehend things.

The only difference was that cheering up called for even greater effort.

'Yes, yes,' she said after a pause. 'I'm delighted . . . only my eyes aren't too good.'

My last conversation with her had been on the day of our departure on one of our regular visits to Paris. In her look it was easy to discern the question that most mothers ask on these occasions: When you come back, will you find me alive?

But after a prolonged stare, she finally put to me the most surprising question of all.

'What?' I said, hoping that I had not heard correctly.

But my hope was in vain.

The Doll repeated what I thought she had said. 'Are you a Frenchman now?'

Later, whenever I remembered this question, instead of becoming familiar it seemed more and more strange, from whatever side I considered it. So clear yet so obscure, childish and timeless at the same time, her words caught me wholly unprepared. In short, they were utterly in her style – comprehension and non-comprehension at the same time, joined in life and in death.

And so I answered her question only now, as she lay in a coffin, white, with a little red on her cheeks, entirely the Doll in a toy box.

As I looked at her, it seemed that she had been preparing for years to make this leap. She had put on a little make-up as if for a final performance, but her manner was still the same, and the essence of her question was still the same, about the replacement of a mother, though now articulated in the pretentious phrases 'Mother France' or 'Mother Albania'.

Of course, my reply would be to her, to myself, and to some other dimension that might sit in judgement over us, as my father did long ago in his famous trials.

I wanted to tell her that she could no longer complain of a lack of consideration. She was the centre of attention in the role of the deceased, the main protagonist of antique tragedy, as students throughout the world learn.

People now encircled her, just like in the theatre of Tirana that she had perhaps visited in secret without imagining that one day she would take the stage herself to assume her role in a three-thousand-year-old drama.

Here they were, intimates and strangers, each more important than the other, all wearing expressions of grief, half of them in silence, some in black Borsalinos. Some speaking foreign languages.

For your sake, the actors of the National Theatre lowered their resounding voices, which you so adored. For they all knew that you were about to set off to meet your husband in Tirana's western cemetery, just as you had once come to him as a bride in the distant year of 1933. And he, like then, might say to you, 'Have you come to me, Doll?'

In these last moments I will try to avoid things that are difficult for you, like that matter of the darkness from which we all emerge. Or the other one, the darkness to which we are all going.

At least for these minutes I would like to reassure you once more that the misunderstandings between us did not hinder me in any way, but were perhaps more necessary than any kind of rapport. Because, as I've tried to explain to you so many times, a gift may manifest itself in its very opposite – that is as an absence of something rather than an abundance.

And I recalled the Russian poet on that cold night in Paris as he told me how on his last trip to Moscow a woman had spat at him in the street, just like that, for no reason . . . *ponyimayesh* . . . for no reason, in the street one evening . . . a woman wrapped in a shawl, as Mother Russia, *Matushka Rus*, is usually depicted . . . *ponyimayesh* . . . on the posters in November. And he asked her . . . 'Why . . . ? What have I done to you . . . ? Why did you spit at me . . . ?' While she, not taking her eyes off him . . . threatening . . . mysterious . . . gave no answer.

13

M Y SENSE that something was missing from
my portrait of the Doll became clearer
when the architect dealing with the reconstruction of the house phoned from Gjirokastra
with the news that he had discovered its secret
entrance.

I felt unprepared for this news and found myself
lost for encouraging words that wouldn't disap-
point him.

'Yesterday afternoon,' he continued cheerfully,
'we were working on the east wing, and

suddenly . . . you see . . . we were astonished . . . quite amazed . . . you see . . . ?'

'Yes, yes,' I replied, after a time, but feeling my sluggish response was justified. After all, nobody could be thrilled to discover that the house where they spent the first seventeen years of their life has a secret entrance, and still less when the news is relayed with cries of delighted astonishment and endless *you sees* from the architect in charge of renovation.

He talked on while I hunted for banal phrases in reply, and came up with the most useless question imaginable: 'Was it a secret entrance or an exit . . . ?'

'What?' he cried. 'Entrance or exit? . . . Hmm, what a strange question . . . really strange.'

I rather regretted my interruption and conceded that it might be considered both at once, and I felt the anxiety pass from him to me.

It was a strange kind of unease, for few people will ever have to worry whether a secret entrance or exit is a good sign for a house or not.

This consternation, a kind of obscure misgiving, clung to me even after I hung up.

A secret way in . . . or way out . . . what's there to worry about? I thought.

And yet my apprehension would not go away.

I had known the architect before the house was destroyed.

'I come from Lunatics' Lane,' he had said to me with a cheerful face, as if telling me he had a degree from Oxford.

We laughed, as we later did whenever we recalled that first meeting. The fact that we both came from this famous little street would surely help us to understand one another.

We were in complete harmony until the day when the house, as if playing some great trick on us, caught fire during the repairs and burned to the ground.

I appointed the same architect for the house's reconstruction, and everything was as previously:

degree, Oxford, our harmony. As before, we understood each other totally, down to the word 'air raid', which we used quite nonchalantly, simultaneously.

When we met for the first time beside the ruins, he noticed my incredulity at what I saw and used the very words that were in my mind . . . 'It looks like there's been an air raid, doesn't it.'

'Precisely,' I replied. And he told me that the houses of Gjirokastra burned in this way, as if bombed from the air, unlike all other houses in the world. The collapse of the fortress-like walls had caused general amazement.

The architect explained that the cruel blow our house had suffered was the equivalent of two large bombs dropped from a heavy British bomber. The house was roofed with stone slabs which, when the supporting rafters burned away, collapsed into the house with all their appalling weight.

One might say that the Kadare house was bombed by its own roof – that is, by itself.

And then in that unforgettable year, 1999,

something happened that never occurred in World War Two. Waves of NATO aircraft flew across the Adriatic to bomb Serbia. The fire in our house was at about this time. In my mind, the idea of destruction had been associated with air raids for so long that I could easily imagine a British bomber peeling off from its squadron and, flying over Gjirokastra like a character in some fairy tale from my childhood, seeking out our house, on which to drop those two long-awaited bombs.

But as so often happens, a misfortune brings its own consolation, and thanks to this mishap we found the secret entrance to our house, which might otherwise have remained undetected.

It was something much more than an entrance, something deeper than any secret. It seemed to me to offer a vital code to interpret everything, including the riddle of the Doll.

This is what ran through my mind as Helen and I travelled to Gjirokastra. The architect had insisted that she should come too, because my friends there had prepared some kind of surprise for her . . .

I did not stop to consider what this surprise might be, because the whole event could only be a surprise, starting with the house, which was both itself and no longer itself.

The house was to have a second life now, something never granted to people. The rooms, corridors, staircases and carved ceilings would experience a resurrection, while the non-rooms, which had never been rooms before, would embark on a second life without ever having had a first.

I tried to put this jumble out of my mind, for it seemed to me more esoteric than the philosophies of Pythagoras and Plato put together.

And so, pestered by a little group of friends, we arrived at the western gate. The architect pushed open the door and we passed through into the entrance hall, which led to another door that led into another hall where the internal staircase was.

A third door opened into the eastern yard with its external stairs.

All together we climbed this stone staircase, which still had no protecting rail, to the upper floor. I saw my guides glance at one another with the special look of people who share a secret understanding, and noticed they were careful to keep Helena at the front of our procession. I remembered the surprise that the architect had mentioned, but in my unfocused state of mind I forgot it once again.

The cortège led by Helena reached the top of the stairs, and suddenly, in the midst of a silence of the sort created by whispers of 'Watch out! Be careful!', an old song burst forth from a large number of male chests.

People hurried up the staircase to see what was happening. The sight was breathtaking. In the big first-floor corridor stood a row of men in fustanellas, assembled in a formal semicircle, singing an old wedding song in resonant voices.

Helena stood immobile in front of them, captivated.

The song was for her. It was a famous Gjirokastra song, perhaps the oldest of all wedding songs, and she was the bride.

> *Bride, here where you set foot, may you also*
> *lose your teeth.*

In other words: Bride, here where you enter, may you remain for the rest of your life.

The singers did not take their dark and minatory eyes away from her.

She had been many years in coming, but had finally arrived. It was too late to rescue her, or to change anything. She was being told bluntly: You will never leave here.

This must be a misunderstanding, a kind of mirage of a wedding from another era. It was the wrong bride, and I instinctively wanted to cry out: Stop this dangerous play-acting, curtain down!

Meanwhile, Helena had acquired an extraordinary kind of beauty, as if she wanted to do well by the house.

Everything around was grim, threatening.

I wanted to say that it was no longer the house that it had been, and it had no rights over a bride who had married elsewhere.

I wanted to say something more, about the regrets the old house still somehow held, its long wait, and its pointless spite, but at that moment the song abruptly stopped, as is usual with this kind of music, as if the performers' breath had been taken away.

The company now descended the stairs with the same haste as when they had come up, as if fleeing a danger zone. I managed to pass through them to take the still-dazed Helena by the hand and say to her 'Be careful!' as, almost in a panic, she came down the stairs without a rail.

At the foot of the staircase, as we walked towards the gate, I thought it might be better for us to leave by the secret door, but I remembered that I still had no idea where this door might be, nor could I glimpse the architect anywhere, and the feeling that overcame me was nothing other than a continuation of the perplexity of long ago.

Paris, April 2013

THE LEOPAR

The leopard is one of Harvill's hist
an imprimatur of the highest qual
around the world.

When The Harvill Press was fo
former Foreign Office colleagues M
Marjorie Villiers (hence Har-vill),
express intention of rebuilding cultu
the Second World War. As their first c
'The editors believe that by producing
important books they are helping to
barriers, which at present are still big
change of ideas between people who
frontiers.' The press went on to publish f
ferent languages, with highlights includ
Tomasi di Lampedusa's *The Leopard,* Bo
Doctor Zhivago, José Saramago's *Blindness,*
The Rings of Saturn, Henning Mankell's *
and Haruki Murakami's *Norwegian Woo*

...RD

...oric colophons and
...ity literature from

...unded in 1946 by
...anya Harari and
...it was with the
...ral bridges after
...atalogue set out:
...g translations of
...o overcome the
...to close inter-
...are divided by
...rom many dif-
...ling Giuseppe
...ris Pasternak's
...W. G. Sebald's
...Faceless Killers
...d.

Summit

Cyclops

...nity
...ies